Thunderlands

To Peter O'Hare

with best wishes.

your old friend,

Stewart Birt

Thunderlands

Stewart Bint

Also by Stewart Bint

Acknowledgements

Thank you to Miika Hannila and the team at Creativia.

Special thanks to my wife Sue, son Chris, and daughter Charlotte.

And thanks to my good friend, fellow novelist DM Cain, for her unstinting enthusiasm and encouragement.

For
Marc Freebrey

Contents

Foreword

A bolt of lightning. A crack of thunder. The lingering smell of ozone in the highly-charged air.

And the world has changed forever.

Or has it? Maybe the world we knew is still exactly the same... *somewhere else*. In the precise moment that the thunderbolt boomed, what if a portal had opened up and sucked us through? And we're now in a different world in a parallel universe.

In the wink of an eye we've been transported to a world we don't know. Even though it looks the same on the surface, there's just a hint that all may not quite be what it seems beneath. Even the most ordinary things may be just a touch out of kilter.

We've left our old lands behind, where things usually happen for a logical reason and with an express purpose. We now reside in strange new lands, where the unpredictable becomes the norm... where the plain ridiculous is lurking just under the skin of reality.

Welcome to the Thunderlands.

A collection of 21 short stories ranging from the sublime to the unforgivably ridiculous, including The Trial Of Santa Claus, where the jovial guy in red faces charges of cruelty to children; The Twitter Bully sees an online cyber bully get his come-uppance in a particularly grotesque way; and "Hello Dear" in which the ghost of an elderly lady keeps appearing to a career woman.

Others include A Timely Murder, where a man goes to unusually severe lengths to ensure he is convicted of a crime; The Wind Of Fire, featuring a space traveller with three eyes and a two-foot-long trunk who finds a mysterious book on a dead world; and Harvey Looks For A Friend, telling of a young ghost desperately seeking someone to play with.

And then we have Ree – The Troll Of Dingleay, a nonsense poem written with a lot of help from the pupils of Huncote Community Primary School, in Leicestershire, UK.

The book puts humanity on trial for our offences, in some cases literally. Many of the stories are a study of human nature, even if all the characters aren't, strictly speaking, human, examining themes such as greed, lust, gluttony and plenty of other deadly sins, with a widely differing series of characters and settings.

Stewart Bint, Desford, Leicestershire, Saturday, 21st April, 2018

"Hello, Dear"

"Hello, dear."

The words usually instilled a warm calm in her, ever since she'd first heard them and seen the old lady in the tartan skirt and grey cardigan. The kind, slightly wrinkled face was almost as familiar as her own. It had been nearly 20 years since the woman started appearing to her, always smiling.

A knowing smile.

"That's the beauty of being a ghost," Jenny had often thought to herself during the old lady's visits. "Never to get any older, always staying the same."

"Hello, dear," she said back to the ever-smiling woman. But this time she wasn't so confident. Her life was now happy and complete, so why was the old lady here? Was it a terrible disaster she had come to forewarn about?

However, Jenny's life had been very different when she saw her the first time. It was only six months after her marriage to Malcolm, and already things were starting to go wrong.

"You can forgive him for his affair," the old lady had told her. "He will never stray again, I promise you."

"But how can you be so sure?" Jenny had asked.

"I'm sure. Trust me." The old woman gave her a gentle nod and slowly vanished into thin air. Jenny stood rooted to the spot. Ten minutes earlier she had been viciously hoovering the floor, pulling the cleaner backwards and forwards with quick, angry jerks. How could Malcolm do this to her? How could he wreck her life like this? Didn't he know how much she loved him? Why had he done this? And with *her*, of all people? His *secretary*, for goodness sake.

"Hello, dear." The words spoken right by her ear, so quietly, yet clearly audible above the roar of the vacuum cleaner, took her totally by surprise. She was alone in the house, so who was talking to her?

Jenny whirled round and saw her standing there: early 70s, grey hair pulled back tightly into a bun, smiling sweetly. But she wasn't quite whole, the green floral wallpaper of Jenny's living room was visible straight through her. Jenny gasped in amazement and horror.

"Hello, dear," the old woman said again. "Please don't be frightened. I've come to help you."

But Jenny was frozen to the spot, unable to move, unable to utter a sound.

"W-who are y-you?" she managed to stammer eventually, her mind whirling, completely incapable of rational thought. After all, what could be rational about a 70-year-old woman who wasn't quite whole, wasn't quite real, standing – no, *floating* – in her living room?

"Please don't be scared of me. I'm not going to hurt you."

She never stayed more than a few seconds. Just enough time to tell Jenny what she had to know. Always that gentle nod, the smile widening ever so slightly as she faded into nothing. Jenny was never frightened after that first time.

It had been during the second visit, a year later, when the old woman said to look upon her as her guardian angel. "The path of your life will not always be easy or smooth, my dear, and although I will be here to help you, I can't always tell you which route to choose."

"But why are you helping me like this? Who are you?"

The old woman ignored the questions. "You're wondering whether to take the new job with Harrison Bonham Associates," she said. "Or to stay with Sprackleys and take the promotion they're offering."

Jenny nodded, dumbly. The old lady was spot on. Jenny had been agonising over her decision after telling Helen Sprackley she was leaving the small, but growing, Public Relations consultancy to join a much larger, rival, operation.

The increased package had been swift in coming: a ten per-cent rise in salary, plus an upgrading of her car, an extra week's holiday and an increase in her pension entitlements. Clearly an offer not to be sniffed at. But Harrison Bonham Associates was a well-established consultancy with a wonderful reputation; one of the best in the business, in fact. With that name on her CV the PR world would be her oyster in a couple of years. She could go to any consultancy in the land, more than likely as a board director, probably as Managing Director. But how would that sit with plans to start a family?

And that was when the old woman came a third time, to find her firmly ensconced as Sprackleys Managing Director; Helen Sprackley having taken on the role of chairman after Jenny had opted to stay with the company.

"You're wondering whether your career can fit hand-in-glove with raising a family. Well, it will. Go ahead, my dear, start your family as you want to. It's the right thing to do. If you don't, you'll always regret it."

With Jenny's excellent salary at Sprackleys and Malcolm also earning good money as a well-connected fashion photographer, she knew they could easily afford the best child-care. But how would she feel when the baby actually came along? Would she want to stay at home all the time to look after it? Would her career matter so much to her then? It certainly mattered now, but would it in the future? Would her priorities change?

And so the elderly woman came a fourth time. "I just don't know what to do," Jenny told her.

"I know, my dear, I know. It's hard for you," the woman said. "You're worried that if you leave the agency you'll be bored at home, and that Gemma will only occupy your time for so many years. But you can always return to your industry later, when Gemma's older, when she's at school. Someone with your experience will always find work."

The fifth visit was, indeed, when Gemma was starting school. Helen Sprackley offered Jenny her old job back as Managing Director; Jenny's replacement having moved on to Harrison Bonham Associates. Funny how things work out, Jenny told herself.

This time the agonising was over whether to run her own part-time business from home, so she would be there when Gemma came in from school; so she would be there when Gemma was ill; so she could be sure of not missing school sports days and plays. The offer of MD was very tempting, but would be full-time. Working from home would keep her mind occupied; keep her hand in and provide her with a degree of financial independence while ensuring she was always there for Gemma. When Gemma needed her.

And so Jenny gave birth again. Not to a baby this time, but to Jennifer Radcliffe Communications.

"Hello, dear." The old woman appeared to her on the first day of business, smiled sweetly and said: "You've done the right thing," before vanishing. Never before had a visit been so brief.

And so the old woman's appearances stopped. The years flew past. Jenny and Malcolm doted on Gemma. Every six months Malcolm would take professional pictures of her, and the growing portfolio catalogued her young life, from the moments after her birth, through her captivating smile and first steps, to her first day at school in grey pinafore dress, white shirt and red cardigan, first sports day – when she broke the tape by winning the 50 metres sprint, and of course, all her birthday parties.

Gemma was six when her brother Dominic came along. Jenny had wondered whether the old woman would appear again when she and Malcolm had been discussing whether to try for another child. Both of them knew that if they were to have another baby it had to be now, before they, and Gemma for that matter, grew any older. After all, Jenny's body clock was ticking away relentlessly. She was now 35 and Malcolm was 41.

But there were no appearances. Jenny began to worry about making her mind up. All her major life decisions had been influenced by the old woman's comforting, reassuring presence and words. Malcolm just thought she was a good decision-maker. But this time he sensed she was having trouble.

However, he knew better than to push her. If pushed, she fell into a stubborn rut and sulked with him for days. Eventually she did make up her mind, as Dominic was testament to.

Over the years she had longed to tell Malcolm about their very welcome supernatural visitor – her guardian angel – but he didn't believe in ghosts. And after all, she told herself, it was her secret, shared alone with the old woman, whoever she was. And so she never told him.

She often wondered if she would ever hear those once-familiar words again. Yet here they were, almost 20 years after she first heard them and 10 years since the last time.

A chill of pleasure ran down her spine as she turned from her computer screen to see that familiar face smiling back at her.

"Hello, dear," she replied, using the old woman's regular greeting back to her, unable to control the feelings of intense pleasure which tingled through her body before changing to those of doubt.

"Don't worry, my dear," said the old woman. Uncanny. It was almost as if she were reading Jenny's thoughts about disaster. "We won't be seeing each other for a very long time to come, and I didn't want you to forget me, that's all."

Jenny was almost crying. "Of course I won't forget you," she sobbed. "You've helped me so much." The smile widened, just as before, and the old lady faded into nothing.

And so the years passed by. Gemma and Dominic grew up and had families of their own, providing Malcolm and Jenny with a clutch of much-loved grandchildren. Jenny's PR firm also grew to a very respectable size, employing over 50 people. She had all but retired in her early fifties, only taking on a part-time role as Chairman. And, exactly as the old woman forecast, Malcolm never strayed again.

Yes, her life was happy and complete.

One day the sound of hoovering suddenly came from the living room. Malcolm was out, so who was in the house with her? And who would be hoovering, for goodness sake?

Her heart pounded as she trod silently down the hall and opened the door, peering cautiously inside. There was a young girl viciously hoovering, pulling the cleaner backwards and forwards with quick, angry jerks.

But the girl and her hoover weren't quite whole, weren't quite real. Jenny could see the recently hung light red flock wallpaper and newly fitted dado rail right through her.

And the girl was *floating*.

Suddenly Jenny understood. Now she realised why the old woman's face had always seemed so familiar, right from the very first time she saw her.

She strode up behind the girl, the vacuuming masking the sound of her footsteps.

"Hello, dear," she said.

The Trial Of Santa Claus

Now, I'd always thought of Santa Claus as a kindly old man who loved children. So it came as a shock to find he was appearing in court. And the charges fair made me gasp: cruelty to children, they were. Who'd have believed it?

Looking back almost 12 months to that amazing day when I sat in on Santa Claus's trial, I can see it all again as clearly as if it were yesterday. I suppose I shall never really know just how it happened. All I know is that it did happen.

I'm a newspaper reporter in a small English town struggling to make my way in the world and one of my regular jobs is to cover the local magistrates court. The magistrates sit on a Thursday in the Town Hall dispensing justice to assorted thieves, villains and other rogues.

On this particular day the magistrates and I were all finding it hard to keep awake. The cases were boring, the defendants were putting up boring alibis, and even the court officials looked bored.

The presiding magistrate, Mrs Eleanor McHarris, was just peering over the top of her fancy horn-rimmed spectacles at the latest chap in the dock, when her whole body started sort of weaving about. I stared at her, totally fascinated.

Her pale, blue-rinsed hair was streaming out all around her head as if she were caught in a wind coming at her from all sides. The top and bottom parts of her face were blowing to the left, while the middle, the bit that held her nose and cheeks, swayed to the right.

I felt as if I wanted to cry out, but stopped myself in time. Mrs McHarris was a right tartar if people made a noise in her courtroom. I looked at the others, but it appeared they couldn't see anything amiss. The clerk to the court was droning on in that monotonous voice of his, reading a list of charges to the defendant; the prosecuting solicitor was eager to get to his feet to put the case against the man in the dock...no-one noticed that Mrs McHarris was coming apart at the seams.

And it wasn't just Mrs McHarris going haywire. A weird type of greyish-white mist began swirling before my eyes. Goodness knows where it came from, it just suddenly appeared. For a few seconds it blocked out Mrs McHarris and the rest of the courtroom. But I could still hear the boring old clerk reading the charges. I couldn't actually hear what he was saying, but his voice penetrated through the haze like a muffled fog horn.

Sanity was restored the next moment. Or at least I thought it was.

I found myself still staring at the swirling mist, but at least I was able to put it into perspective now. I was staring through the window at the thick blanket of snow falling outside.

I looked back at Mrs McHarris. Sanity disappeared again. She'd stopped her strange weaving about, but somehow she looked different. I blinked. Okaaay. I must be seeing things, I told myself, as her appearance began to register in my mind. No wonder she looked different. Most of that blue-rinse was now tucked up inside a long black pointed cap, with only a few wisps hanging loosely past her ears and trickling on to her shoulders.

Her grim tweed jacket wasn't there any longer, either. Instead, a heavy black shawl sporting a long fringe was draped around her. And those fancy horn-rimmed glasses stretched out sideways and curled up to a point, giving the impression of a flying bat.

The only thing that remained the same about her was that she was still peering over the top of the spectacles which perched precariously on the end of her nose. The nose: why, even that was longer than it had been before. Wasn't it?

And when she spoke...well; gone was the supercilious educated, plummy accent. The words which cascaded out came in a thin, whining cackle. I realised at once that something was dreadfully wrong. I'm quick like that, you see. Yes, it was very wrong. The clerk to the court should be saying those things, not the presiding magistrate.

"You've heard the charges against you, Santa Claus, how do you plead, guilty or not guilty?"

The immediate answer from the dock was booming, almost boisterous: "Why, not guilty, of course, Madam." Now, that didn't sound for one second like the sort of voice the frail young man who'd been standing there just a few seconds ago should have had. It had rich, deep tones, as if it belonged to a jolly, middle-aged, or even old, man.

And wait a minute. She'd said Santa Claus. What the deuce was going on?

I tore my gaze from the ugly old hag (uglier and older, anyway) that Mrs McHarris had become and stared across to the dock. The wimpish-looking wally charged with some insignificant breach of the law was no longer there.

Instead, there stood a man with a myriad laugh-lines creasing the skin around his eyes and the lower part of his face was concealed by a bushy white beard. He was about six feet tall, and a bright red tunic encased his more than ample girth. White hair flowed out on to his shoulders from under a red drooping cap.

Santa Claus! How in tarnation had he got there?

I gave up trying to work out what had happened. I could have speculated all day and still been a million miles from the truth. There! With my mind wandering I'd missed some of the court procedure. The prosecuting lawyer was getting to his feet, ready to put his case to Mrs McHarris.

"Madam," I heard him say. "Santa Claus has denied the charges against him, namely cruelty to children. I shall now proceed to show you just why Santa Claus is guilty of the offences as charged."

At least the solicitor looked the same, I thought. Or did he? I'd seen old Chatstock in action in this courtroom many times, soberly attired in an immaculate dark suit. But somehow that suit now looked tatty and well-worn. And the man himself appeared to stoop a little, whereas he normally pulled himself up to his full height when beginning a case.

Mrs McHarris gave an irritated wave of her claw-like hand. "Yes, yes, do get on with it, Mr Chatstock."

He coughed apologetically. "Call the prosecution witness, Miss Anne McGuigan."

Miss Anne McGuigan was duly called and took her place in the witness box.

As she went through the formalities of pledging to tell the truth, the whole truth and nothing but the truth, I stared at her, trying to remember where I'd seen her before. Of course, it had been in this very courtroom a few months ago. Like I say, I'm quick like that.

She's a social worker and had again been involved in a case of cruelty to children. She looked to be about 35 years old and her stern face gave her a general haughty appearance. Yet, like Mrs McHarris and old Chatstock, there were some definite changes in her. The long, thin nose was even longer and thinner than I remembered it, and the tight, bloodless lips indicated where the mean mouth slashed its course above her pointed chin.

"Miss McGuigan," old Chatstock was saying. "Will you tell the court in your own words exactly what effect Father Christmas's actions have been having on children?"

She flashed steely grey eyes across the room to Santa Claus. "With pleasure. Why, it broke my heart to see those poor children sobbing, the way they were. That man has completely wrecked the spirit of Christmas. It can never be the same again as long as he's out there, supposed to be bringing joy and happiness to all those poor little souls, when all he does is bring misery and heartache."

"Yes, yes, quite, Miss McGuigan, quite. But can you tell us please, exactly what it is he's said to have done?"

"*Said* to have done?" She seemed to spit the words with utter contempt. Especially the first one. "There's no 'said' about it. He did it all right. It was him who came down all those chimneys on Christmas morning, no-one else."

I didn't think it'd be long before Mrs McHarris threw in her ten pen'orth. And I was right. I'm quick like that, you see.

"There is no law as far as I am aware against Santa Claus coming down people's chimneys on Christmas morning," she said.

Old Chatstock turned to face her. "I'm sure you're right, Madam, but I must ask you to forgive Miss McGuigan for her unaccustomed outburst. It's just that she's seen the results of Santa Claus's doings at first hand, and she feels very strongly about it all."

He turned again to his witness. "Miss McGuigan, you really must refrain from making comments about what happened. If you could just stick to the facts, please."

The mean little mouth turned sulky. "Oh, alright then. It's just that what he's done makes my blood boil." Miss McGuigan swiftly moved on to what was asked of her before the magistrate or her lawyer could rebuke her again. "The happiness amongst children on Christmas morning over the past few years has been very limited. They've opened the presents Santa brought them and their little eyes have lit up with wonder and awe. That's something I've seen on numerous occasions in my line of work. The present is new and shiny and of course they love it.

"But when they get together and compare presents, each child feels their friends' gifts are always better than their own. They start to ask each other how much the presents cost, and they become discontented. That feeling quickly grows to a fierce jealousy, and in a very short time their sweet innocence becomes a lingering hate and resentment that they haven't got a bigger, better, more expensive gift. If that isn't cruel to the poor little dears, upsetting them like that, then I don't know what is."

Miss McGuigan continued in the same vein for another half hour, and was followed by a succession of children all saying what Christmas meant to them.

And the answers they gave…well:

"It means presents."

"Lots to eat."

"I think it's about some geezer who died and we remember the day he died."

"I like the chocolates."

"Dad gets drunk and Mum cries."

"It means I can get a new computer. The one Santa brought me last year isn't as good as Robin's, so I want a better one."

"It's Santa's birthday, but instead of us giving him presents he gives us things instead."

"Billy's present always cost more than mine, so I like to break it when he lets me play with it."

As a journalist I've become hardened and cynical to some of the nonsense people put forward in a courtroom, but when Santa started to defend himself it was all I could do to sniff back a tear.

"Madam." His booming voice echoed around the ancient timbers. "I can't deny that what much of the prosecution says is true. The spirit of Christmas – its true meaning – has been wrecked. Some children turn bitter and twisted when they see a better toy than theirs, or one which was more expensive, and it does rob them of their innocence at a painfully early age. Oh yes, I agree that is wrong. But you can't blame me for it. I'm afraid Mankind's progress through time has become tarnished. The further He goes and the more He gets, the more He wants." Santa shook his head sadly.

"I know if I'm found guilty I shall spend some time in prison, but that's not the reason for my stout defence and complete denial of the charges laid against me, Madam. I'm opening my heart to you with feelings and thoughts I've had for a long time. But it wasn't until I was arrested that it brought home to me just how bad things are getting and how the world has changed in a few short decades.

"Whatever happened to the idyllic Christmases when families went to church together on Christmas morning, and it was a time for rejoicing because our Saviour had come to Earth on that day two thousand years before?

"He came to save the world, to show its people the way forward. If ever it's possible for Him to come again, the time is now, for Mankind has strayed from the path He showed them. The journey has become cluttered with material possessions that people prefer to the simple ways of Our Lord.

"They've let grasp and greed cloud their lives and they've lost sight of the true road ahead. They over-eat in comfort while others go hungry. They have warm beds while others shiver in the cold. There's no compassion left in the world. Everyone strives for something better and they always want the greener grass on the other side.

"You can't hold me responsible for that. If anyone's being cruel to children, it's their parents, for giving them too many material possessions and not enough love and spirituality. Children grow up with everything handed to them and with no appreciation of values – either material values, or more importantly, spiritual values."

At that stage old Chatstock finally managed to chip in. I could see he'd been itching to for a couple of minutes. "But if that's the case why do you continue to visit these children year after year? Wouldn't it be better for you to ignore the world for a time?"

Santa shook his wise old head, a sad smile pulling at his lips. "No, I couldn't do that. I've always visited the children over Christmas Eve night and Christmas morning and see no reason to change now.

"If Mankind wants to tread this particular path, who am I to say no?

"But remember this – the spirit of Christmas is still there for those who choose to seek it. For that reason, if you find me not guilty, Christmas will continue to come to the world every year, despite the self-destructive path a minority are taking. But think of this – can the world survive if we no longer celebrate the birth of its saviour? I put it to you, that it cannot.

"The world is what people have made it. And people are what the world has made them."

He stopped speaking and gently lowered himself into his seat.

Mrs McHarris stood up. "If that's all you wish to say, Santa Claus, then we'll retire to consider our verdict."

Now, it wasn't the first time I'd dozed off for a few moments while waiting for the magistrates to come back with their decision. I awoke with a start when Mrs McHarris tapped her gavel sharply on its block. For a couple of seconds I looked at her in astonishment. Her pointed cap was gone, so was the fringed shawl. Also back was the grim tweed jacket.

And Santa was gone. His place taken again by the wimpish wally.

It took a few more seconds for everything to sink in. Then I laughed under my breath. It looked as if I wouldn't get to hear the verdict on Santa Claus after all.

Through the ensuing days I tried to work out just what had happened in that courtroom and what the verdict could possibly be. I'm quite good at predicting which way the magistrates will decide, but in this case I didn't have a clue.

Santa had said he'd go to prison if he were found guilty. And that didn't bear thinking about. Just imagine all those disappointed faces if he didn't pay them a visit.

But when Christmas morning dawned all my worries were over. Santa came as usual, and as far as I know he called on everyone. I reckon he must have been found not guilty. What was it he said? Oh yes: "But remember this – the spirit of Christmas is still there for those who choose to seek it. For that reason, if you find me not guilty, Christmas will continue to come to the world every year, despite the self-destructive path a minority are taking. But think of this – can the world survive if we no longer celebrate the birth of its saviour? I put it to you, that it cannot."

I think that says it all, don't you?

Oh...and just in case you think I dreamed the whole thing; no, no, no. I've still got the shorthand notes I made during that day I covered the trial of Santa Claus.

The Fourth Wish

The ugly features of Reginald Todd were even more grotesque when reflected in the convex outer wall of the old Aladdin-style lamp. His red bulbous nose looked to be all of four inches wide. But at least the tiny weasel eyes, set too close together, appeared to be stretched to a more acceptable distance. Yellow, uneven teeth showed through thick smiling lips as he gazed down at the lamp cradled in his hands.

"Well, what d'you know?" he muttered. It had only been a couple of minutes since his metal-detector unearthed the grimy lamp in a ditch, but his greedy mind was already thinking of its value in pounds and pence. "An antique dealer or junk shop might give me something for you."

Gently he started to rub the grime away to get a clearer view of his face reflected in the brass, increasing the pressure with his finger all the time. Suddenly a wisp of smoke shot from the lamp's spout, starting to thicken and solidify before his eyes.

With a yell of surprise he dropped the lamp as if it had instantly become red hot, but the smoke continued to pour from it, and within a few seconds the swirling mist had taken the form of a fully-grown man.

Todd stumbled backwards, staring aghast at the six-foot-tall, dark-skinned figure, looking resplendent in a golden flowing robe and red fez. The newcomer's arms were folded across his chest and he bowed low before straightening up to look directly into Todd's eyes. Ivory white teeth glinted through a jet black beard when he smiled and spoke.

"Greeting, My Lord. What is it you wish?"

Todd shook his head, dumbly. "Who are you?" he managed to stammer eventually.

"I am the Genie of the Lamp," the stranger told him. I've come to grant you three wishes. I have to obey the Master of the Lamp."

Todd's mind did a double somersault. A genie to grant him wishes! It was beyond his wildest dreams.

"What can you give me?" he demanded.

"Why, Master…anything your heart desires."

Todd began thinking of possibilities. Then the Genie spoke again. "There's no rush, Master. Take your time if you want to think how to make the most of your opportunities."

"No." Todd came to an immediate decision. He knew exactly what he wanted, so why wait? "I want money, incredible wealth. Give me a 40-roomed mansion and £100-million in the bank."

He had hardly finished speaking when there was a crash of thunder and the world darkened. A couple of seconds later the light restored and Todd found himself standing in front of the most imposing house he had ever seen. Marble steps led up to an Oak front door, with windows stretching away on both sides.

"I'm rich, I'm rich," he cried, his weasel eyes taking in the glory of his new home. Then he thought of his ugly face and how it repelled people wherever he went. "Can you change my appearance?"

The Genie nodded silently. Instantly Todd knew what his second wish would be. "Make me handsome," he ordered. "The most handsome man on Earth."

A boom of thunder rolled in again and Todd found himself spinning helplessly through an infinite blackness. A searing pain tore at his face, remoulding the flesh with fingers of fire. The agony was so intense that it wrenched an involuntary cry from his lips before he realised it was over. He was standing again in the driveway to his mansion, and apart from a slight tingling in his cheeks he felt as if nothing had transpired.

"Well?" he demanded, looking across at the Genie. "What's happened?"

For an answer the Genie plucked a mirror out of empty air. Todd snatched it, staring in amazement at the perfectly formed Adonis features looking back at him from the glass with piercing blue eyes topping high, prominent cheekbones. He looked in awe at the slightly aquiline nose that was considerably smaller than the one which had protruded from the train wreck of a face he would have been looking at just seconds earlier.

Parting the full, sensuous lips revealed perfect, even white teeth. His smile was dazzling. And replacing the thin, straggly, mousy hair, a sheer cornucopia of blond locks the colour of ripened corn, topped this artist's canvas of male perfection.

"Excellent," he mused, fingering his new face. Then a scowl creased the smooth, high brow. "But I won't stay like this, will I?" He turned angrily to the Genie. "You've given me all this, but it won't last forever. I'll grow old, lose my looks and eventually die. Then what good will me wealth be? Unless... yes, I know. My third wish is to be immortal, to live forever, never aging from this moment."

Once more, darkness stole the daylight for a few seconds, accompanied by the now familiar thunderclap, and he felt a tremor pass through his body as the Genie's forces did their work on his molecules and DNA, freezing them in a permanent state of agelessness.

But Todd was still not satisfied. "I've no control over people," he grumbled. "No real power. No way of making them do what I want."

He slapped his forehead in a somewhat theatrical gesture. "That's what I should have asked for: absolute power. Look at the power you've got. I've no power at all, but you can rule people – you could rule the world with the forces you can conjure up. I may be immortal now and wealthy, but I've no real power over people. That's what I really want.

"I wish I were a Genie and have the power to..."

Todd's ravings were cut short by a fourth thunderclap, and when he recovered his senses he found himself sitting cross-legged in a confined space, with a huge face looking down at him through a hole in the roof of wherever he had suddenly come to.

With a shock he realised it was the Genie's face, grinning.

"Nothing has given me greater pleasure in granting you an extra wish, Master. I now have your riches and immortality on Earth, and you, Reginald Todd, have my life as a Genie, just as you wished for.

"I waited in that lamp for a thousand years."

He stooped to pick it up, and slamming the lid down with Todd inside, he hurled it back into the ditch.

"I do hope you won't have to wait so long to demonstrate your new-found power."

The Growing Thing

The Growing Thing grew a little more and squelched its way through the bushes near to a group of children who continued their game, blissfully unaware of its existence.

The sun beat down mercilessly, as it is prone to do over Los Angeles in mid-August. The Growing Thing didn't like the heat and took shelter whenever it could amidst the trees and bushes. It had discovered some shade in the San Gabriel Mountains and the Angeles National Forest, but opted to stay in Griffith Park where the food supply was a little more plentiful.

And if there were one vice The Growing Thing could say it had succumbed to, it was greed. It liked its food and because of the heat found it necessary to partake of its favourite morsels a little more often. The sun tended to dry it out and slow it down, sapping its energy. It needed more food to replenish its strength. Gastric juices flowed deep inside its slimy, slippery body in anticipation of the forthcoming meal. The single red eye towards the top of the vibrating, glutinous mass glared out balefully as it stalked a victim.

A wail of sheer pleasure broke from its slobbering lips several cycles above the range of a human ear.

The children's dog heard it, though, and stopped dead in his tracks. He let go of the stick in his mouth and turned to stare at the bushes. Stiffening his back legs he dropped the front part of his body to the ground, ready to spring forwards. The Growing Thing howled an invitation for the dog to come and find it.

"Corky, come back," squealed Virginia Vesey. But if the dog heard his young mistress, he disobeyed her. He stopped a couple of metres from the bushes, barking loudly. To The Growing Thing the pitch of the labrador's bark was painfully low and vibrated throughout its every fibre.

The last Virginia saw of her pet was when he nosed his way into the bushes. With a shout of triumph The Growing Thing dropped over Corky, completely smothering him. The dog died with hardly a whimper, his body being scooped up and thrust between the wet, greasy jaws almost immediately. Bones crunched as the marrow was sucked out of them, and powerful teeth ripped into flesh, tearing it to shreds. The Growing Thing shuddered ecstatically, its waning strength already returning. Muscles deep in its stomach got to work on the dog's pelt, moving it this way and that, rolling the skin and fur into a tight ball. Then, with almost no effort, it expelled the ball onto the grass.

Virginia pushed through the bushes on her hands and knees in search of her pet. Her eyes came to rest on The Growing Thing. A silent scream rose quickly. She opened her mouth, but her throat remained locked solid. No matter how she tried she couldn't utter a sound.

Had The Growing Thing been capable of smiling, it would have done so at that moment. Having devoured its starter, here was the main course right on time. The lower jaw unhooked and the green rubbery lips folded themselves over Virginia's sweet and tender five-year-old body.

Power flooded back into The Growing Thing with every swallow. And within the two minutes it took to finish its meal it had grown another inch taller and inch wider. It relished the succulent living food that was so plentiful on this planet, especially the smaller juicy morsels such as the one it could still taste. They were the best, the ones to pick should there be a choice. It had noticed how the passing of time left its mark on the living food, coarsening the meat, making it tough and stringy, but still edible and nourishing.

The Growing Thing was thousands of times bigger than it had been when it crashed on this primitive world. Its taste buds had quickly become accustomed to the ever-changing delicacies it needed to keep alive, from tiny segments of a blade of grass through to lumps of soil, worms, then insects, birds, cats and latterly dogs and humans.

Its brain scrambled incomprehensively trying to understand the life forms it encountered on Earth, but decided that none was too intelligent, certainly not enough to feel pain as The Growing Thing, knew it. And so it had no qualms, felt no pangs of conscience, in simply devouring whatever took its fancy. It was lost on an alien world, frantically trying to survive in the best way it knew.

Virginia's friends stood by the bushes waiting for her to come out. The Growing Thing sensed increasing panic amongst them as their calls went unheeded.

Four-year-old Damien decided to go in and have a look. The Growing Thing then used a trick it had carried off successfully before. By standing stock still and pressing itself up to the shrubbery it could pass a not-too-close scrutiny unnoticed, with its green and brown scaly body merging chameleon-like into the background.

Damien cast a cursory glance into the clearing and didn't even spot the regurgitated undigestible remains of Virginia piled up in the undergrowth.

"She's gone," he said as he backed out, knocking pieces of soil and leaves from his clothes. "So's Corky."

Ellie-May thought she knew what had happened. "I bet they've gone out the other side somewhere and are hiding from us. Let's go and look for them."

The five children scampered round the other side of the bushes and trees and hurried off down the path. It would soon be time to go home for tea.

* * *

Mr Vesey put the 'phone down and turned to his wife, the worried look on his face saying it all. He glanced at the clock. "Two and a half hours since anyone's seen her. Barbie says she crawled into the bushes to look for Corky and must have run out the other side."

Mrs Vesey sobbed into her husband's shoulder. "Where on Earth can she be?"

"Don't fret. Corky's with her. He won't let anyone harm her."

"Phil, I'm so worried."

"Look, let's give her another half hour, then we'll get the police to look for her."

"But it's getting dark out there, Phil, and all her friends are home now." Sue-Jane's voice began to crack. "Something's happened to her, I just know it has."

Phil ran a hand lovingly down Sue-Jane's shining yellow hair. "She'll be alright."

"Ring Lieutenant Bolderelli, please, Phil. Now."

* * *

Lieutenant Bolderelli stared aghast at the grisly sight which lay illuminated at the end of his torch beam. "God Almighty, will you look at that."

Sergeant Leahman peered equally aghast at the tattered pieces of bloodstained cloth, pale empty skin and the matted blonde scalp rolled up in three neat piles. He clutched his stomach and retched noisily. Bolderelli felt like doing the same.

"In all my years on the force..." His voice trailed away as he slowly shook his head. He didn't need to say he had never seen anything like it for Leahman to understand perfectly what he meant. "You'd better get back to the car, Leahman. Radio in for forensics to get down here. And tell them not to let anything drop to the Veseys yet. Not until we're sure."

Leahman didn't trust himself to speak without retching – or worse – so simply answered by nodding silently to the back of Bolderelli's head, before scuttling away from the claustrophobic bushes to gulp in great lungfulls of air.

What was left of Virginia Vesey was delicately packed into three plastic bags and taken back to the pathology lab for extensive analysis.

Leahman lost track of time as he waited in an ante-room just down the passage from where two of the city's top forensic scientists were busy with their microscopes and chemicals carrying out almost every known test on the pathetic remains. The six empty plastic cups in the waste-bin alongside the sergeant's seat had earlier contained strong black coffee from the vending machine, and indicated that his stomach was feeling a little stronger now.

He finished re-reading the evening newspaper for the third time before glancing at his digital watch.

"How much longer?" he half whispered to himself. Then the double doors swung open. "Doctor Stanton..." he rose to meet the advancing figure.

Doctor Stanton was in his late forties and his most distinguishing feature was a mane of silver-grey hair, its bold waves neatly parted on the right, falling more than an inch below his collar. It had been said that Doctor Stanton cultivated his hair to divert people's gaze away from the large round nose of which he was fashionably self-conscious.

Snugly-fitting grey trousers protruded from below the white gown of which he was in the process of divesting as he came through the door.

"Sorry to have kept you waiting Sergeant." His rapidly delivered and somewhat thinly-sounding words were indicative of a keen, powerful mind. "It's just that we've never come across anything like this before. Not since High School days, anyway."

"High School days?"

Stanton nodded. "Biology classes."

Leahman's large domed forehead creased into furrows. "I'm sorry, Doc, I don't follow."

"Owls," said Stanton, simply.

"Owls?"

"Owls. What do you know about them?"

"Well, nothing really. Except that they come out at night and sleep during the day."

"Is that all?"

"Um…yes."

"What do they eat, for instance?"

"Doctor Stanton, what's this got to do with Virginia Vesey? That is Virginia Vesey in there, isn't it? At least, what's left of her, anyhow?"

Stanton nodded. "It's what's left of her, alright. What's been regurgitated from something's stomach."

Leahman flinched, feeling as if something were in danger of being regurgitated from his own stomach. "What?"

Stanton nodded again. "That's why I asked what you knew about owls. When owls have finished a meal they cough up the parts they can't digest…the pelt and other such stuff, in a neat little ball. It looks as if something's done just the same to that poor little kid."

The sergeant was speechless. "But…but, that's…what?"

"Horrific; impossible…yeah, use whatever hyperbole you like. But it's happened. And the evidence is in there to prove it." Stanton's calm, analytical mind wasn't going to be put off by what he had seen and discovered, however improbable it seemed. He had witnessed death in many forms and could not afford to let his emotions run free.

"There's no doubt about it, Sergeant. The fluid in those remains is some sort of gastric juice which is definitely not human. She was eaten by an animal…God knows what type of animal…which then spat out what you gave me in those plastic bags."

* * *

At the precinct, the Chief Of Police didn't want to believe it, but was forced to accept Doctor Stanton's findings. He had been called in from his home and now briefed his men personally.

"We don't know what we're up against," he said somewhat unnecessarily. "Our scientific boys reckon the thing that killed Virginia Vesey must be some large animal. More tests are being carried out. All we…"

"But Sir." The interruption came from half way back amongst the assembled officers. "What sort of thing is it that could eat a child in this way?"

"When I said we don't know what we're up against, I meant it, Sergeant Traceman. There isn't a lion or tiger or any other man-eating beast missing from any local zoo or circus, and no-one's reported seeing anything like them wandering about.

"As you know, the number of missing people in the city has increased by up to 30 per cent in recent weeks, but no extra bodies have been found, and certainly nothing like the remains of Virginia Vesey have ever been seen before.

"The boffins have done God-knows what tests on those remains and have come up with nothing. They're completely stumped. The fluid found in them is nothing known to science. The nearest resemblance is the gastric juice of an owl, which also spits out the remains of its meals in a similar way to how it appears this creature has done."

"Have the press and television been informed, Sir?"

"Don't be stupid, Officer Schulz. Do you think we want mass hysteria on our hands?"

"But don't you feel people should be told about it? Warned to be on their guard?"

The Chief Of Police nodded miserably. "Yes, I do think they should be told. But not yet. We've got until tomorrow night to find this creature, whatever it is, and kill it. After that I'll have no option but to unleash that hysteria. The army will also be called in then. But until that time, it's in our hands. I want that thing found and destroyed.

"You'll be working in pairs, and as well as your normal service guns you're all being issued with high-powered rifles."

He pointed to the map on the wall and assigned each pair to one area of the city. Finally he turned to face the door at the back of his rostrum, starting to move towards it, before stopping to turn back. "Oh, and ladies and gentlemen, I need hardly say be careful. And good luck."

* * *

Out in the park The Growing Thing felt uneasy. It had returned to the scene of its last meal in the bushes and found to its horror that the remains it had coughed up were gone. This was the first time it had failed to bury the incriminating evidence and now it was worried.

It tried to relax under the moon and stars by regulating its breathing ready for a few hours rest, but sleep eluded it. The single red eye peered all around, searching for any kind of danger. The pupil dilated to its maximum. Now the sun was gone it didn't have to squint against the harsh blinding light. It felt at home in the darkness.

Something else troubled The Growing Thing, too. Something it couldn't understand. It felt a strange nauseating sensation deep within its body, as if its very being were stretching in all directions. It thought for a fleeting moment how happy it had been when it encountered the Earth after its long journey. It had wandered through space like a cosmic Romany until it sensed life teeming across the surface of the green and blue world it had spotted below.

Now it felt different. It had seen the world shrink around it every time the fireball of a sun had risen at the end of a stretch of darkness and every time it had eaten the living food. A change was taking place deep within every cell. Each cell was growing a replica. Every nuclei was dividing and its cytoplasm was splitting into two.

The Growing Thing writhed around in the bushes, thrashing at the leaves and branches – its high-pitched scream dispersing silently into the darkness.

Agonising pain shot through it. The pain every human mother offsets with the pleasure of seeing her offspring emerge from within her.

Its vision blurred and a red mist swam before its eye for a few seconds, which it clamped tightly shut. Fear engulfed it, ordering it to lie still so nothing should find it, nothing should destroy it. The eye opened slowly, tentatively probing the darkness. The vibrating head turned deeper into the clearing, and what The Growing Thing saw caught its breath. It was looking upon itself, or at the very least, another of its own kind, its own race.

The second Growing Thing looked back with equal wonder. It had thought it was alone on this alien world, devoid of any kinship. It couldn't work out what had happened. Perhaps something in that succulent flesh it had eaten earlier was causing it to hallucinate.

The first Growing Thing probed back in its mind. What was causing it to feel like this? Perhaps something in that succulent flesh it had eaten earlier was causing it to hallucinate.

The second Growing Thing remembered the long journey through the endless abyss of space. So did the first Growing Thing. Together they remembered their single shared experiences as one.

While the old Growing Thing fell asleep the young one went off in search of food. It may have its parent's thoughts and memories but it certainly didn't have a full stomach.

* * *

Bolderelli and Leahman had been assigned Griffith Park. Cautiously they made their way towards the bushes where they had found Virginia Vesey's undigested remains, thinking there was no better place to start looking for the creature that had devoured her. There must be some trace of whatever it was that would lead straight to the hungry jaws.

It was Leahman's torch this time which picked out the grisly sight. The sight of The Growing Thing snuggling up in the bushes, sleeping the sleep of the just.

The Growing Thing watched with its single red eye from a safe distance.

It saw the living food pointing long sticks at its parent.

It saw those same sticks spit fire and howl explosions.

It saw angry lead balls tear their way into its parent's body, ripping flesh, pulverising vital organs.

It sensed, rather than saw, the essential life forces stream out of its parent's body, disappearing into nothing. But one thing would be etched forever in its memory. And that was the dreadful dying scream several cycles above the living food's hearing range.

The next morning The Growing Thing was still crying in silent anguish for its lost kin as it vowed revenge on the savages inhabiting this barbaric world. The Growing Thing felt the powerful warmth from the fireball in the sky penetrate its body. It grew a little more and squelched its way into the bushes near a group of children who continued their game, blissfully unaware of its existence.

Money To Burn

Harrison Micklewhite didn't speak a word of Norwegian, and thought it ridiculous that his client should drag him away from his London shop to close their deal aboard the Oslo to Bergen Express.

Granted, it wasn't costing him a penny. His air fare from London to Oslo, the overnight hotel stop, the train ticket and the return flight from Bergen to London, were all coming out of Rupert Templeman-Hyde's seemingly bottomless pocket.

But it had still meant shutting 'White's Philatelics' for two days. He trusted his wife and loved her dearly, but even she had to admit her knowledge of the international stamp world left a lot to be desired.

He obeyed Mr Templeman-Hyde's instructions to the letter and sat in an ordinary compartment until the train trundled through Nittedal Valley 15 miles out of Oslo. Then he set off down the train in search of compartment six in the fourth carriage.

It amazed him how quickly Mr Templeman-Hyde had got to hear that he had acquired the two stamps. It also amazed him that the billionaire should offer £2m for the pair. That was twice their market value, even though they were the only two of their kind in existence.

The telephone conversation between the two men had been brief and to the point. Mr Templeman-Hyde wanted those two stamps and was prepared to pay well for them; for his private collection, he said.

At first Micklewhite wasn't sure. He was a great stamp lover himself, and felt they should be on display somewhere, not locked away depriving the eyes of the world. But when Mr Templeman-Hyde made his cash offer… well.

This was it. Compartment six. The blinds were pulled down inside. Micklewhite tapped hesitantly on the door.

A single answering word, somewhat muffled, came from within. "Ja?"

"Er, Mr Templeman-Hyde…?"

"Ja."

"It's me, Sir. Micklewhite. Harrison Micklewhite. I've got your two stamps." As he spoke, someone brushed against him.

Suddenly the door to the compartment slid open in a swift jerking movement and a huge head shot out, peering up and down the corridor. The florid face turned an even deeper shade of red at the sight of the retreating figure which had walked past Micklewhite a few seconds ago.

Pushing past the stamp dealer, the tall and bulky red-faced giant grabbed the third man by the shoulder, spinning him round, before demanding: "Do you speak English?" The other man spread his hands, seeming to indicate he did not understand.

The giant pushed him away, whirling round to face Micklewhite.

"Mr Templeman-Hyde…" began Micklewhite.

"For God's sake be more careful," the big man said.

"Careful? Why? I don't understand. This is all above board, isn't it, Mr Templeman-Hyde?"

"What? Yes. Yes, of course it is. It's just that I don't want anyone else to …well, let's just say it's a good job that man didn't speak English."

The billionaire seemed to be regaining some semblance of composure.

"You say you have the stamps?" he asked.

Micklewhite nodded. "And you have the money?"

Mr Templeman-Hyde pointed to a leather holdall on the seat. "You may count it if you wish."

He cut short the dealer's protests. "In that case tell me again about the stamps."

Micklewhite pulled an envelope from his breast pocket and carefully extracted two stamps, which he put into the billionaire's outstretched hand.

"The stamps depict the christening of Prince Leopold of Battenburg, in St George's Chapel, Windsor, in 1889. Only four were produced, and now there are only two left. One was destroyed in a fire. A dog chewed up the other one."

"So these are the only two left in the world?" Mr Templeman-Hyde cradled them lovingly in his hand.

"I do hope you'll show them to the public," Micklewhite said. "It would be a tragedy if they were kept for your eyes only."

The billionaire dragged his gaze away from the stamps to look directly into the dealer's eyes.

"Tell me, Mr Micklewhite, the rarer a thing is, the more it is worth, yes?"

Micklewhite nodded.

"And these two stamps together are worth, what, around £1m?"

Again Micklewhite nodded.

Mr Templeman-Hyde's stare was intense, unnerving. "But suppose I only had one? Suppose there was only one of them in the world. How much would that be worth?"

"If there was only one…a stamp with this much history…Prince Leopold…easily £5m. It would be priceless." Micklewhite didn't like the glint his travelling companion's eyes. "Why do you ask?"

For a silent answer, Mr Templeman-Hyde dropped one stamp into his inside pocket, fished out his cigar lighter and calmly burnt the other stamp to a cinder.

A Timely Murder

Looking back after all these years, Bill Hunter knew his plan wouldn't work today, with Facetime, Skype and other forms of instant communication.

But 1982 had been a different kettle of fish altogether.

* * *

It was the waiting that got to Hunter more than anything. He stared around the courtroom, his eyes coming to rest on the door into the ante-chamber, where his future was being decided at that very moment.

The clock took his gaze next. Surely it can't be long now, he thought. Guilty or not guilty…what would the verdict be?

Hunter had often used such periods of waiting to reflect on the pros and cons in his day-to-day life. He was a successful businessman with his own computer company, and his attractive and vivacious wife had kept her looks through her thirties and well into her forties. At 48, Margaret was five years his junior, and it seemed to outsiders that it was the perfect marriage.

But when those observers had gone home from the Hunters' lavish parties and the doors were bolted against the outside world the veneer peeled back, showing the true nature of what lay beneath.

Over the years he had come to accept that the marriage was ended, and even after the children left home it was only held together for appearances. He had had a few flings, and no doubt so had Margaret. He was content to let life keep rolling along like that, but he did draw the line when she dropped the bombshell over breakfast one morning.

"By the way," she had said nonchalantly, while clearing away the marmalade jar and butter dish. "Can you move your easel and paints out of the pastel room tomorrow? I want to clean it in time for the weekend. I've invited someone over."

"Who?"

"Someone I want to spend the weekend with."

"Who?" he insisted.

"You don't know him."

"Him!" Hunter spat the word. "What the hell are you playing at?"

"If you don't shift those things they're going straight in the bin."

And so the wheels were set inexorably in motion. Every weekend after that, Doctor Charles Hine came to stay, and Margaret slept in the pastel room with him.

As the months went by Bill Hunter grew to loathe his wife more and more, and gradually a plan began to form in his mind.

Now, in the courtroom, like a drowning man's life flashing before his eyes, Hunter recalled the details of that fateful night, to check again that there were no flaws. Would the keen legal brains he was contesting see through it?

When he left the office that day he had called cheerily to his secretary. "Right, Sylvia, I'm off. Don't forget I'm in London all day tomorrow for the Datateknik meeting."

Sylvia grinned. "I won't, Mr Hunter. And don't you forget you're in the Grosvenor Court Hotel tonight. I couldn't get you at the Wilton Palace."

But instead of going to London, he drove slowly to the large isolated house he had shared with Margaret for the last 25 years, careful to make sure when he turned in through the gates that no-one saw him.

"I suppose you're 'phoning Debbie tonight?" he asked, as Margaret started gathering up the dinner dishes.

"Of course. Two minutes past two. You should know that without asking."

Every year since their daughter had emigrated to Napier on North Island, New Zealand, Margaret had insisted on telephoning her on her birthday, at the exact moment of her birth: two minutes past one in the afternoon, New Zealand time. That meant getting up at two in the morning English time to make the call.

"Well, don't wake me," he remembered saying, feigning just the right amount of irritability.

"Aren't you going to speak to her?" Margaret sounded aghast.

"Not this year, no. I'll ring her from the office tomorrow morning at around ten. They'll still be awake then." He paused, then added almost as an after-thought: "Oh, don't mention that to her. Let it be a surprise."

* * *

The incessant bleeping of his digital watch alarm snapped him awake at ten minutes to two. Reaching out to the bedside light he could hear Margaret in the neighbouring bedroom as she prepared herself for her big moment. His heart pounded wildly in his heaving chest as the muffled clop of her wooden-soled mules moved past his door, along the landing and down the stairs.

A few moments later he, too, crept down the stairs and could hear Margaret humming softly to herself in the lounge. Hunter silently opened the back door and positioned himself outside the lounge window, pressing his ear to the glass, listening for the first signs that she was talking to their daughter.

"Debbie? Hello, Debbie. It's Mum. Happy birthday, darling. How are you?"

As usual, she sounded excited and was shouting loudly into the telephone. "A party? When? Tonight? How wonderful."

The rest of her words were drowned out beneath the smashing of the window as Hunter hurled a rock through it. In a few deft bounds he was through the back door again, peering cautiously into the lounge.

Margaret was running towards him.

It had to be swift. He knew that. Before she could utter his name.

The 'phone handset lay by the cradle, and he could not afford for Debbie to hear the wrong thing. Such as his name.

Margaret gasped in astonishment, her curious glance taking in his fully-dressed figure. Then she cried out in horror as her eyes fixed on the long-bladed knife in his raised right hand. Desperately he lunged towards her, feeling unconcealed satisfaction when the blade tore through her thin over-wrap and buried itself deep in her heart.

While he was opening the broken window and throwing aside the curtain he could hear Debbie's frantic voice from New Zealand: "Mum? Mum? What's happening? Mum…?"

His Jaguar purred down the country lanes and out on to the main road. He kept glancing down to the dashboard clock as the car increased speed. Eventually he pulled on to a farm track and sprinted the remaining 500 yards to Doctor Hine's cottage. Hunter had not been idle during the weekends Hine spent with Margaret, so it was not without a certain amount of practice that he deftly sprang the lock back on the side door. He had been over this route many times and knew exactly what to do.

First port of call was the grandfather clock in the hall which said ten to three. Gently he eased the pendulum to a halt and wound the hands back to five minutes to two. He pushed the pendulum back into its rhythm, pausing for a couple of seconds to make sure the clock was going again, before he tiptoed up the stairs.

He slowly slipped the bedroom door open about three feet and squeezed through the gap, making his way silently towards the bed and its neighbouring table.

Staring down at the sleeping man he felt a sudden urge to beat him about the head. But he quickly pushed such irrational thoughts firmly out of his mind.

First things first, he thought. Reaching down, he pulled the bedside clock radio's electric plug out. Instantly the back-light faded and the flip-over figures on the digital read-out were stilled.

His mouth hardened, and in one swift movement he kicked over the table, which went down with an almighty clatter.

Hine was awake in a second, sitting up in bed. "What the hell's going on?" The moonlight shining faintly through the thin curtains cast an eerie glow on Hunter's menacing form towering above him.

Hunter didn't respond, but merely froze like a grotesque statue, making sure Hine could not mistake who he was.

"Who...? Good God. Hunter. What are you playing at, man?"

Again, Hunter failed to respond. Just standing there. In the ensuing silence he heard the grandfather clock strike twice. And made a point of glancing at his watch. Six minutes to three. So far, so good.

He hoped Hine had seen and heard enough to be able to remember everything later, and aimed a well-placed fist at the Doctor's jaw. Hine crumpled with a groan and his breath was expelled from his body by another sharp blow, this time to the stomach. Then he sank back, unconscious.

It took Hunter no more than two minutes to reset the pivoted flipover figures on the digital clock radio to two o'clock, and put the grandfather right again.

Two hours later the sleepy night porter at the Grosvenor Court Hotel handed him his room key.

* * *

Prosecuting counsel was merciless in his summing up. "We even have the exact time of the attack," he said, confidently. "As you've heard, Doctor Hine clearly recalls hearing the grandfather clock strike two o'clock, and the plug was pulled out of his bedside clock when the table was knocked over. It had stopped at just gone two. Doctor Hine was most emphatic about both the man and the time. It was the accused, William Hunter, and it was two o'clock.

"The tragic thing is, of course, that that is the exact time Mrs Hunter was murdered during a break-in at their home 30 miles away. That has been corroborated by their daughter. If Mr Hunter had been at home instead of making this assault on Doctor Hine he may have been able to save her. He will have to live with that of the rest of his life.

"Despite Mr Hunter's denial, we have the evidence of the hotel porter who insisted he didn't book in until nearly five o'clock in the morning.

"I put it to you, ladies and gentlemen of the jury, that at two o'clock on the morning in question, William Hunter was not at that hotel, as he claims, but was assaulting Doctor Hine."

Hunter's memories of his movements that night dissolved as the jury trooped back in. He remained standing while the foreman announced their verdict.

Fighting back waves of relief Hunter turned to face the Crown Court judge who announced his sentence.

"William Arthur Hunter, you have been found guilty of a premeditated assault upon the person of Doctor Charles Edward Hine. The court does accept, however, that there was a certain amount of provocation, and, of course, this is your first offence.

"Having said that, though, I have no alternative but to send you to prison for nine months."

The flicker of Hunter's eyelids could have been mistaken for mute anguish. But his thoughts were far from anguished. If ever the ongoing enquiries into Margaret's unsolved murder came a little too close for comfort all he need say was: "Look, Inspector, I have been convicted of another crime at the exact moment my wife was killed."

The Stealer Of Dreams

Wild-Rune stared miserably at the orange streaks tinting the clouds to the west of Banatray. A reddening sky, as the day drew to a close, might delight the shepherds on the slopes of the valley, heralding as it did, a fine summer's day tomorrow, but it only brought despair to Wild-Rune.

Before the next dawn, the night would have to come, and for Wild-Rune the night no longer gave the refreshing sleep it once did. When the sun disappeared behind the tree tops at the edge of the forest across the valley, the darkness would bring its usual assortment of terrors and nightmares.

The village elders were seeing it happen all too often. And they had heard of it happening all over the kingdom. Now they saw the same pattern developing with Wild-Rune. During the first few nights of her illness – for that was how they preferred to speak of it, even though they knew otherwise – her dreams had just been of a half-glimpsed nameless fear. This had relentlessly moved on to unleash a raging world of unimaginable horror where night after night she fell prey to whatever it was that roamed the dark shadows and corners of her mind.

* * *

Monster after monster lurched across her dreamscape, severed hands clawed at her face as she desperately tried to flee, but her legs were so heavy she could barely drag one foot in front of the other. At times she would catch a glimpse of burning red eyes following her every move in the darkness. She didn't know what those eyes belonged to, but she sensed they would tear her apart if she let them come close. With her leaden legs refusing to obey her silent pleas to speed her away, she sensed the owners of those eyes closing in on her.

While her sleeping mind was held in the relentless grip of such night-time terrors, her mother and stepfather were trapped in a nightmare of their own. For them it was the waking nightmare of being powerless to prevent Alee-Brun's only daughter suffering in this way time after time.

In the beginning the dreams were generally calm, simply disturbing her sleep just a couple of times each night. Then the land that would become her nightly home for many weeks, grew increasingly sinister and doom-laden, populated by all manner of malevolent beings. The first time it happened, her piercing scream sliced through the stillness of the dark shortly after midnight. Bran-Rick was awake in an instant, out of bed and running towards his stepdaughter's room.

"What is it?" Alee-Brun's voice was thick and distorted with sleep, as she drowsily pulled herself up, awoken, not by the scream, but by Bran-Rick's sudden movement. By the time she reached her husband's side he was bent over Wild-Rune's bed.

"Wake up, Wild-Rune, you're having a nightmare, that's all." *That's all.* Those words would come back to haunt him in the days – and the nights – to come. But at that time, he felt it was just a simple, one-off nightmare, because Wild-Rune generally slept soundly, although in recent days she had spoken in passing about half-remembered dreams.

He reached towards her, gently shaking her shoulder as violent spasms wracked her body.

At first that night Wild-Rune had slept soundly, her untroubled breathing was slow, gentle and calm. Then, gradually as the night wore on, she sensed something was not as it should be and the dream began to unfold. One moment she was walking through the pasture lands that bordered the village. The next, she felt herself becoming trapped in the dreamscape of her growing nightmare, running swiftly through an unfamiliar forest pursued by something equally unknown. She had to get away, couldn't let it catch her, couldn't let it devour her, couldn't let it tear her limb from limb, which she knew was all it wanted to do. It was close behind her, gaining inch by inch as they both plunged headlong through the thickly packed trees whose branches intertwined high overhead, blocking out the sun, bringing an almost eternal dusk to the forest floor.

Her clothes were unfamiliar, too. Gone were her favourite, crudely sewn leather dress and knee-length laced boots, replaced with a tattered shirt and shorts. Branches lashed at her face and arms, and small, sharp stones and twigs bit into the soles of her bare feet as she hurtled on through the oppressive half-light. Suddenly memories came flooding back and the land no longer seemed quite so unfamiliar. Directly in front of her stood the shattered remnants of a once tall and proud Shagbark Hickory whose trunk had been cleft in two by a lightning bolt. In her waking hours this strange and brutal land would be just half-remembered and banished to those mysterious fragments of the mind that tried to hide things it didn't want to remember. But now, somehow, she knew the geography of the forest she found herself in as she realised she had been here before.

Those other times, though, were in dreams, not a nightmare like this. Those other times she had spent walking peacefully along the forest trail, only occasionally being aware of something moving parallel with her through the trees.

Disturbing, but not frightening. It was a deer, she had told herself confidently, just a deer. Not this time, though. This was no deer she was running from, this was something evil that wished her immeasurable harm. That was why she was running. But her newly-remembered knowledge of the forest may be able to help her.

She knew that just a few metres to the left of the shattered Hickory a clearing would open up in front of her, stretching away for about a hundred metres in all directions. And there was something in the centre of the clearing that would help her escape from her ever-nearing pursuer.

If only she could get there in time, but it would be a close-run thing. She could hear something slithering through the undergrowth close behind her. Too close. Gaining. How far to the clearing now? How far to the centre of the clearing and safety?

She burst through the blanket of trees into achingly bright sunlight, and there, 50 metres away, stood the craggy ten-foot-high monolithic rock which she hoped would prove to be her salvation. Half way across the intervening space she risked a glance over her shoulder. And saw her pursuer for the first time.

That was when the piercing scream erupted from her sleeping body, waking her stepfather.

Her eyes were still getting used to the sudden onslaught of the sun after emerging into the glade from the dim half-light of the forest, but her nightmare swiftly adjusted the light to compensate. Whatever had given birth to the nightmare wanted to ensure she could see her pursuer in all its horrific malevolence. And what she saw sent a thrill of pure terror coursing through her dreamscape persona, opening the floodgates for adrenalin to swamp her bloodstream. Fear spilled from her in waves, drawn along the nearby ley line until finding its target behind the remnants of the Shagbark Hickory. The few seconds she stared at her pursuer were long enough for several more waves of fear to flow from her into the ley line.

Towering 20 metres above her were two pointed faces each of which appeared to be connected to necks at least two feet in diameter, merging about half way to the ground into one four-foot-wide trunk of a body. The body was sidewinding along the ground towards her. The underside of the two-headed snake was a pale bluish-white, which contrasted with the dark blue scales above. Four tiny piercing eyes, two on each side of both leathery, scaly faces, glinted redly above gaping mouths which revealed wickedly pointed fangs bearing down on her. Despite belonging to one body, each head seemed to be acting independently because they both struck at the same time, colliding with each other. Knocked off their target, the two sets of fangs flashed harmlessly past Wild-Rune's neck.

It gave her the few seconds she needed to reach the safety of the monolith. Why she was safe there she didn't know. She just knew she would be. Flinging her arms out she grasped the rock and found herself soaking wet, crawling out of a river that flowed along a valley floor. Snapping at her heels were dozens of tiny, needlelike teeth in the mouths of hundreds of small fish that swarmed through the water towards her. Scrambling onto the bank she turned to look back at the water. The fish were emerging onto the land, the split in their tails getting longer, turning each fish's tail into a pair of short, stubby legs. Suddenly a fish launched itself at her, latching onto her shoulder, burying its teeth deep into her flesh. Gasping with pain inflicted by the dozens of tiny pinpricks she instinctively lashed out at it, shaking her body, desperately trying to throw it off.

In the waking world Bandrick's hand was gently shaking that same shoulder.

She stabbed at the fish, but its teeth were firmly embedded. Grabbing its head, she squeezed with all her might, pulling upwards at the same time. The teeth came clear of her skin, dripping with her blood, and in the next instant the head exploded in her hand, showering her face in wet, sticky, stinking goo.

She scrambled further up the bank, her feet slipping in the mud. There, in front of her was the shattered Hickory, meaning that just nearby was the craggy, monolithic rock to give her protection.

If only she could get there in time, but it would be a close-run thing. The fish were waddling after her, surprisingly fast on their squat tail-legs. Getting closer. Gaining. How far to the Hickory now? Would she see the rock when she got there? How far to the rock and safety?

Many more times that night unnameable creatures caught up with her just seconds before she grasped the rock and was catapulted into some other frantic chase.

Sometimes the speed at which she was running surprised her. Her bare feet flashed unerringly across the land – grass, rock, gravel, mud

– carrying her mile after mile just out of reach of her relentless pursuers. Desperately she looked for the broken Hickory. And every time it was almost, tantalisingly, just within reach when she was finally overhauled, and teeth would sink into her, or claw-like hands with twisted rasping nails would start to pull her down into the very depths of hell. Each time fear flowed from her along the path of the ley line to its target behind the tree, before the tips of her outstretched fingers brushed the monolith, giving temporary, fleeting safety.

Sometimes her legs would be leaden and, try as she might, she could barely move them, her head frantically looking in every direction for any sign of the horror she knew could only be seconds away.

Fear was now her only emotion. It was fear that sent adrenalin coursing through her veins. It was fear that held Wild-Rune captive night after night, spiralling her ever deeper into inconsolable despair.

And then, just before dawn each morning, the nightly horror reached its climax. The fangs would be drooling just inches from her heels. The disembodied hands, dripping blood, clawed at her back. Spiders dropped with a sickly plop onto her head, crawling through her hair and into her ears, up her nostrils, forcing their way into her mouth, their tireless legs prying at her tightly clamped eyelids. She could smell the hot, fetid breath of the owners of the myriad of red eyes as they surrounded her, cutting off all avenues of escape, closing in slowly, slowly, slowly, biding their time, waiting to rip her to shreds, to devour her limb by limb. Her stubborn feet refusing to move as if trapped in a sea of molasses, sucking her ever deeper into their swirling depths.

Wild-Rune would be thrashing uncontrollably on her bed, her honey blonde hair matted and soaked with sweat.

And each night just before the nightmares ended, Wild-Rune would catch sight of a girl standing behind the Hickory. She looked a little older than Wild-Rune, probably four or five years older. The dreadful white pallor of her skin contrasted starkly with the deep ruby red lips which slowly gaped open to reveal a black tongue that snaked out and lay to rest on her chin. The girl behind the tree then raised her arms to embrace the now tangible flow of fear emanating from Wild-Rune's frantic dream persona. It rushed along the ley line, growing in strength and intensity, taking its power from the ley, stretching itself out before flowing between the girl's outstretched arms and into her mouth. A long, slow sigh escaped the girl's lips as the lustre of her pure white skin became just a fraction brighter than it had been moments earlier. A renewed sheen gave her chestnut hair a richer tint and added glow. The hair also looked a little thicker and a little longer, while the glint in her hazel eyes was one of victory.

As the girl behind the tree dropped to her haunches, seemingly satisfied and replenished, Wild-Rune's mind left the forest dreamscape and returned to her tortured body. Now back in her bed, her wild writhing stopped. Her head sank back to the pillow and her sleep became free of nightmares. It was restless and disturbed, but sleep nevertheless, and held her for those fleeting moments until the first ray of sunshine pierced the gloom around her bed and she awoke drained and exhausted. Day after day the high cheekbones which accentuated her tanned oval face appeared just a little more prominent as the skin below them sank into an ever-deepening hollow. The once shining azure eyes grew dull, listless and unfocused.

The only consolation Bran-Rick, Alee-Brun and Wild-Rune could take was that the elders said the torment would pass eventually. "The illness is temporary," Fore-Site had told them when they sought advice from the village Shamen after the third night. "It's a terrible thing to happen to one so young, but you must take comfort from knowing that at 14 her nightmares won't be as developed as those of someone even just two years older."

The Shamen's sightless eyes betrayed no hint of the anguish she felt for Wild-Rune, knowing that her words were empty and hollow, remembering that terrible night 70 years ago, when at the age of 16, she too, first became a victim of the Stealer Of Dreams.

Silent Witness

Ben crouched under the table. Hoping he would not be seen. He knew he ought to do something to stop it. But his courage deserted him. After all, he was only very small. And the masked man was very big.

Again the knife descended and Ben heard a dying gasp.

* * *

"Two stab wounds," the first detective said. "One to the heart and one to a lung."

"He must have surprised a burglar," observed the second detective. "The dining room window's been smashed. He probably came in and caught the thief red-handed."

The first detective glanced down at the body again. "So much for have-a-go-heroes," he mused, somewhat contemptuously. Suddenly he caught sight of Ben cowering beneath the table.

"Well, well, what do we have here?" Come on, boy, come on out. It's alright, no-one's going to hurt you."

Ben was still trembling. But there was something kind about the policeman's voice. Something Ben liked and trusted. He waved his tail, inching his way out. The policeman bent down and swept the little poodle into his arms. Ben's tongue shot out, covering the detective's face in sloppy licks.

"Okay, okay," grinned the lawman, holding the struggling dog at arm's length, and then putting him down. He mopped his face with his handkerchief. The grin faded as a thought crossed his mind, and he regarded the dog with a frown.

"Say, little fella, you must have seen who did this. Pity you can't tell us."

Ben knew who had done it, alright. The man had been masked, but Ben didn't need to see his face. He knew the man's scent. It was the same man who came in from next door every Thursday night when his master was out playing darts.

The same man who went upstairs with his master's wife and didn't come down again for two hours.

Oh, yes, Ben knew who had done it, alright.

What was it the policeman had said? "Pity you can't tell us." But Ben could tell them. It would defy the laws of nature, but Ben felt he had to do it.

Countless memories spun through his mind, instilled from the many lifetimes he had spent on Earth.

Sometimes he had been a man, sometimes a woman. Sometimes a beast of the field. Now, in his present incarnation he was Ben, the poodle. A witness to his master's murder. A deep sense of outrage welled up inside him. If he didn't expose the sadistic killer who had murdered for the love of his master's wife, the man would get away with it.

Somehow Ben had to talk, to tell the policeman who had done it. His sad brown eyes locked on to the second detective's, holding his gaze. He summoned every ounce of strength he had, calling on deep forgotten specks of magic from the dawn of time to give voice to his canine tongue. He opened his mouth and began. But all that met the policeman's ears was a monotonous rumble.

The first detective looked at Ben in astonishment. "Good grief," he said. "They're normally such yapping little creatures. That's a very deep bark you've got there, little fella.

"Why... what's the matter with your paw?"

Ben's left front paw had shot out, pointing stiffly at the wall.

The second detective patted his head. "My, but you're noisy. You're quite a barker, aren't you?"

The words seemed to strike a chord in the first lawman. His eyes followed the direction of the dog's outstretched paw. "He's pointing next door." The detective turned to his colleague. "And what were those words you used? 'Quite a barker,' you said."

He consulted his notes. "The next door neighbour's a Mr Barker. Paul Barker."

If dogs could smile, Ben would have done so. He trotted off happily towards his dinner bowl, tail flapping from side to side.

Oh yes, he'd put the finger on Mr Barker alright.

The Wind Of Fire

The scorched book caught Zinzibar's attention as soon as he waddled through the archway into the great hall. It was lying on a pile of rubble on the mosaic tiles. Its cover was red, and from where he stood about five metres away, it looked to be made of plastic.

The wall on the far side of the arena had collapsed at some time in the dim and distant past, and now a watery sun poured delicate rays through where it had once towered firm and strong.

Zinzibar wrinkled his two-foot-long trunk in distaste. His three eyes strained to the edge of their stalks, surveying the wreckage and decay around him. His left uppermost tentacle shot out and gingerly rubbed the surface of the book.

He decided it wasn't plastic, even though it had that same peculiar shiny hue; it was a type of coated cardboard.

Its edges were blackened, as if someone had either rescued it from a fire, or flames had licked curiously around it without consuming it.

He turned back the cover, and both his hearts missed a beat. There was writing inside. It was just a series of meaningless squiggles to him, but he was convinced that, as before, on other worlds, the scholars back at the spacecraft would be able to translate it. Their knowledge of such hieroglyphics was unequalled throughout the universe.

Excitedly he scooped it up, dropping it into his pouch. His eye stalks wavered while he probed every dusty nook and cranny for other such treasures.

When that drew a blank he scuttled back outside, wrapping his tentacles around his thick, scaly body in a self-indulgent ecstatic hug. In all his travels he had never found anything like this book. He was always the one who returned from the surface of a planet empty tentacled. But not this time, he thought. This time he would be the hero. Perhaps the secrets enclosed in the book's pages would reveal what had happened to this once-thriving world.

He recalled the wave of euphoria which spread over the gigantic spacecraft when their instruments picked out this uncharted planet. Exploration was always a welcome break from the endless months of flight.

But the headiness slowly deflated as the ship broke through the clouds and passed low over the surface. Looking through the observation ports it was obvious that the planet had once been teeming with life. But all that was left now of its sprawling cities were ruined, flattened buildings. An instrument scan showed no form of intelligent carbon-based life anywhere. The scholars deduced that some great tragedy had befallen its people.

The readouts and computer screens revealed a higher than usual level of radiation in the atmosphere, and again the scholars were called upon for deductions.

They nodded their wise old heads in unison. Yes, they said, it was probably the result of some nuclear holocaust many hundreds of years ago. They would know better, they added, when they could analyse some of the vegetation that clung thickly to the land.

Zinzibar hugged himself even tighter as he raced back to the ship with his prize. Wouldn't it be wonderful, he thought, if his find showed just what had happened?

It was some weeks before the scholars could break the language sufficiently to read the book. But when they were ready they addressed the gathered multitude from the ship's stage.

"It seems to be a diary," they explained to the hushed crowd. "A diary covering several years, as if the writer were afraid to commit too much to paper, or as if it were the only book he had, and paper was scarce."

Zinzibar found three passages particularly fascinating, reading them over and over again until he could recite them by heart.

"Where I was, it seemed like a wind of fire. A hurricane that burned everything in its path. I could feel it coming as I slammed the door of my shelter shut. I only made it inside with seconds to spare.

"For two days I listened to my radio, hearing the horrors of what had happened. The superpowers had wiped each other out: the nuclear holocaust was complete. Suddenly the radio stopped and I lost touch with the outside world. I was afraid to venture out, but my six-month food supply dwindled, and I had no choice.

"What a strange, unrecognisable world was waiting when I cautiously drew back the bolts and stepped through the door. It was summer, and mid-day, and yet the landscape was bathed in an ethereal twilight, and an icy wind roared across the moorland."

Another passage towards the back of the book held Zinzibar's attention even more than the opening one. He guessed it was written several years later.

"Not only is the world changing fast, but so are its people; if indeed, we can still be called people. At first I suppose I was afraid to notice it in myself, but it must have been there.

"As well as experiencing genetic mutations in new-born babies, we elders are growing more horrifically deformed as each day passes. Our skin is becoming tougher, almost like the bark of a tree. I do believe we're mutating into a new species to adapt to the wreckage of our world.

"My arms are growing in length. Only two years ago they fell to just below my knees. Now they're almost to my ankles. My fingers are fusing together to form pincers, and my nose no longer simply rests on my chin, but seems to be making for my chest."

Zinzibar marvelled at the similarities. Judging from the descriptions in the diary the people of this world looked much like his race did now, and they appeared to have evolved along similar lines.

He thought back to pictures he had seen of his ancestors prior to their holocaust, before his own world, the beautiful green Earth, had been shattered by war between North Korea and the West.

Those pictures showed strange, ugly creatures with two arms and two legs, small button noses and only two eyes, horrible smooth skin; and instead of the coarse stubbly growth like his own splendid outcrop they had tiny amounts of thin, fine hair, sprouting from just the top of their heads.

Perhaps before the people of the unknown world had undergone their swift evolution, they, too, had been monsters like his ancestors on Earth.

He re-read the final sentence of the ancient diary:

"I'm worried. There's a strange new trouble at large across our land. It threatens our very existence."

Zinzibar delicately closed the book. So many similarities between the fate of this world and Earth. The one big difference being that the Earth people had survived. This race seemed to have survived the aftermath of the explosion, only to perish many generations later at the hands of some new, unknown force.

He waddled off towards the restroom, hoping in both his hearts that Mankind wasn't plunging towards the same destiny.

Ground Control

His hands trembled as he pulled the joystick with all the force he could muster.

Sweat trickled from his brow.

Sirens wailed.

Lights flashed on the complex instrument bank.

He didn't need the altimeter needle to tell him the ground was rushing up to meet him. His stomach churned as he stared in a detached, fascinated horror at the landscape which bucked and kicked beyond the confines of the cockpit.

A voice crackled urgently through his headphones. "For goodness sake, man, pull up, you're getting in a dive."

"What do you think I'm trying to do?" he snapped into the helmet microphone, straining back deeply into the padded seat, muscles taut, fingers white as he gripped the joystick. Slowly the horizon levelled out and the green countryside began to fall away.

The klaxons still blared like a mournful banshee. And still the lights winked incessantly, telling him the main engine had gone.

The whole affair had begun with a black dot which seemed to suddenly materialise. One moment the infinite blue sky had been marked with just a few fleeting clouds. Then it was there. Full of menace. Hurtling towards him. The first he knew of it was when the sweeping arm on his radar monitor picked it out at the two o'clock position. He had quickly shifted his gaze from the instruments to the four layers of acrylic plastic making up the cockpit windshield with its 12 titanium retainer fittings to strengthen against bird strikes.

At first nothing was there and he had to glance at the radar again to make sure he hadn't been deceived. He hadn't. There it was. Inching its way towards him.

Suddenly the screen showed another dot breaking away from the first. This one moving much faster. A missile. And he was its target.

"GhostWalk Two to ground control," he had said as calmly as he could. "I'm under attack. Taking evasive action."

He narrowed his eyes to combat the sun while scanning the heavens. Even the anti-glare coating struggled to fully combat the dazzling brilliance when viewed head on. Then he saw it.

The black dot was growing bigger all the time.

"I've got visual contact." His voice rose as more and more adrenalin pumped mercilessly through his system. "It looks like a heat-seeking air-to-air."

He hauled the control lever around at the last second and the missile flashed harmlessly past. But he knew he was not out of the woods yet. Not by a long way.

Wildly his head flicked from side to side as he hunted for the deadly missile. The landscape banked through a 90-degree turn and he caught sight of the missile changing its own course.

"It's coming back for another go."

The voice of ground control had been silent until he told them that. They knew his full attention would be focused on evading the missile. Now the controller seemed to think his advice might come in handy. "Can't you get a shot at it, or at least fire a missile to decoy it away from you?"

"Turning now to try." He dragged the joystick sharply to his left, watching as the missile slipped past again. "It's not easy, you know."

Fighting to put his voice back on a more controlled level: "That was the last thing I...."

His world turned upside down in a blinding flash and deafening roar. Almost every warning light sprang into action and emergency sirens assailed his ears.

The event horizon twisted and turned. One moment above him, the next below. The joystick waggled freely for a few seconds until his grip became firmer with his efforts to regain control.

"Mayday, mayday, mayday, I've been hit. It's taken the primary engine."

His eyes scanned a particular section of the instruments. "Secondary engine's cut in, but it's damaged, too."

He could hear ground control screaming back at him, but the constant wailing of the sirens drowned out the words. The altimeter hurtled round showing exactly how fast the fields below were coming up to greet him.

His arms shook violently with the strain, and after what seemed a lifetime the ground returned to its proper orientation. A long sigh escaped his lips as he allowed himself the luxury of relaxing for a second.

Then the voice raised to a shout, fighting to be heard above the banshee: "Come in GhostWalk Two, what's happening?"

"It must have clipped me, I reckon, but it's taken the primary engine. I'm going to have to come down."

He peered forward as if to get a better view of the fields, his hands flashing across the controls, flicking switches and jabbing keys. He took one last look at the instruments before giving the windshield his undivided attention. Treetops whisked dangerously close as the outside world started to tremble and tilt again.

"The secondary engine's about had it," he yelled hoarsely. "It's now or never!"

As he drank in the heady sight ahead the last tree disappeared beneath him. Mile after mile of beautiful unbroken moorland. Luscious greenery stretching away into infinity. He became almost punch-drunk. Not far now. Just a few more metres and those lights would flash like crazy telling him he'd done it. But right now the rapidly increasing grating of metal on metal told him the secondary engine was straining to the limits of its capability.

A glance at the altimeter. Twenty-five metres. Back to the grass. There was a farmhouse ahead. Approaching fast. Back to the altimeter. Ten metres.

He pushed the joystick forward in a final frantic effort to beat the farmhouse, to give maximum power to the reverse thrusters before he hit it. The screaming engine reached a crescendo and the rocketing countryside beyond his window began to slow down. But not in time. He braced instinctively, waiting for the crash as the farmhouse rushed towards him.

When the crash came with its sickening, earth-spinning thud and deafening explosion, time seemed to slow down. The nose of the prototype GhostWalk fighter ploughed through the front of the building showering brick, wood and stone in all directions.

As his seat bucked and rocked, the last thing he saw before clamping his eyes tightly shut were two people ahead of him. A middle aged man and woman, staring aghast as the object of their destruction tore into their bodies, blood and gore splattering against the unforgiving acrylic. But those fittings held.

A powerful whiplashing jerk brought his crazy cascading world to an abrupt halt.

Seconds passed before he risked opening one eye, and what he saw caused him to smile broadly. The outside world beyond the window was quiet and unmoving.

He heard a door opening somewhere away to his right and a hand reached into the training simulator to help unbuckle the seat belt. The hand's owner grinned at him. "At least you weren't blown up in mid-air this time."

He looked into the mocking face above him and grinned back. "Yes, it was a bit better, wasn't it? But I still reckon I need a few more sessions in this thing before we take the real GhostWalk up. She's still not responding exactly as I'd like."

Malfunction

Foreword:

The unique thing about Malfunction and the short story that follows it in this collection, Ashday's Child, is that they were written as completely standalone tales, but when I came to write my full-length novel, Timeshaft, I saw how I could link them and extend their storylines.

As I started to interweave the plots they quickly became the absolute lifeblood of Timeshaft.

There are two ways you can enjoy these two stories – either read them independently of Timeshaft, as separate tales, or skip them as individual tales and simply read Timeshaft.

However, I've found many people like to read them before Timeshaft, just to see if they can work out the link. And I can safely say that no-one has pulled out the right connection.

So, there's a challenge for you, should you decide to accept it!

Malfunction

Hearing the first bleep of the vidlink, Lloyd Bradman looked up irritably from the 3D holo-image in the corner.

"Right in the middle of Alpha-Zero again."

"Why don't you switch it to dormant while the programme's on?" asked his wife, frowning as she tried to listen to the soap opera's leading actor.

"Because the calls may be important."

"They never are," she muttered under her breath.

Bradman swivelled the synthetic hide seat on its single leg and jabbed at one of a dozen buttons indented in the chair arm. The 400-square-millimetre computer interfacing screen on the wall sprang to life, framing the craggy features of Walter Redbrick, the CEO of Australia's leading energy company, Datateknik.

Bradman became instantly alert, and the soap opera's octophonic sound died away in response to another jab at the control console.

"Walter, what...?"

"Lloyd!" Now it was Heather Bradman's turn to display irritation. She touched a similar control in her own chair to bring a degree of volume back to the holo-programme, where a freighter was just blasting off from a space station with a crescendo of noise from its hyper-boosted engines.

The face on the vidlink wrinkled in protest at the octo's assault on his ears.

"Lloyd, we've got a situation." Redbrick's voice was loud to combat the holocast. "I need to see you right away."

Bradman shot a laser-sharp glance at his wife as the spacecraft banked away from the revolving satellite and headed on its way to the caletonium mining colony deep in the remote star system of Pegasus Four. It was Bradman's favourite soap; a futuristic story of the Alpha-Zero space station, floating on a major intergalactic flight path, offering sanctuary for weary tourists and freighter pilots. Five evenings a week the overpaid cast could be seen on the 3D holo-systems in almost all Darwin homes, playing out their tale of everyday space folk.

A jab at another button paused the live show as his mind snapped to more serious matters now, light years away from such far-fetched escapism nonsense.

"What is it, Walter, what's happened?" He stared deeply at his boss's image, and was sure the slightly overlong, wavy hair was a shade greyer than when they had both left the seafront office that afternoon.

"There's been a malfunction in the main reactor at the Macdonnell Conversion Plant." Redbrick's voice sounded urgent, intense; his face drawn. Bradman sensed he was being let into the news gently; that there was worse to come.

And there was.

"The other reactors went into automatic overdrive to compensate, but the computer didn't realise anything was wrong," Redbrick told him. "Each of the secondary reactors slowly built up to critical level, stealing more and more power from the crippled one, until it ran dry and exploded."

Bradman's silence spoke volumes.

And it was a full ten seconds, which seemed like a lifetime, before Redbrick spoke again. "It sparked off a chain reaction. They went up one after the other. There's nothing left of the site." His voice trailed away helplessly.

Bradman swallowed hard. "Is Alice Springs all right?" The Macdonnell Conversion Plant owed its name to being sited partly underground and partly inside a mountain in the Macdonnell range, 240 miles South West of Alice Springs in the Great Australian Outback.

Redbrick nodded. "It's laid waste an area of about 150 square miles, but the town's okay."

"At least that's something. When did it happen?"

"Twenty minutes ago. We've just finished running the telemetry readout. That's how we know what caused it. It's all there, down to the precise second the malfunction occurred in the first reactor and the gradual build up to critical point in the others." Redbrick's voice was now barely more than a whisper, and despite the powerful air-conditioning in his office the communicator clearly showed rivulets of sweat flowing down his face.

Bradman's jaw dropped limply as he drank in the significance of what he had just learned. "I'm on my way over," he said.

Redbrick nodded silently and broke the connection.

Bradman swivelled away from the blank screen and stared unseeingly at the space-craft on the frozen holocast.

Heather reached across and squeezed his arm. "It's not your fault, is it, Lloyd—the malfunction?"

A far-away look overtook his eyes, his thoughts elsewhere; trying to piece together what could have possibly gone wrong in what he had believed was a failsafe operation. Two malfunctions at the same time were inconceivable, yet from what Redbrick had told him there must have been two: the original one in the main reactor—in his mind's eye he traced the link back to the central processing core—then there was the warning system which should have alerted the operators immediately. Even if they had not been watching their systems the audio alarm should have cut in long before the other reactors reached anywhere near critical point.

There was no way such a build-up could go unnoticed. He and two Datateknik engineers had devised the energy conversion process and spent many months perfecting it, installing it and constantly monitoring it.

Unless... and he gave voice to his feelings: "Sabotage."

Heather's eyes widened in horror as her hand, still resting on his arm, closed its grip painfully. "Sabotage?" she whispered. "Do you really think so?"

Bradman pulled his arm away, gingerly rubbing the livid white spots left by her fingers. "I don't know yet," he snapped. "It's just a thought at the moment."

The venom in his outburst died and he reached gently for his wife's hand. "I'm sorry," he said quietly.

She smiled and nodded. "Don't worry, I understand. You'd better go."

Quickly he rolled down his shirt-sleeves, donned a jacket and hurried out of the apartment to the elevator. While he was being whisked down the 28 floors his thoughts went out to the conversion plant's ten late-shift workers; to their wives who would now be widows, and to the children without fathers. All because of a malfunction in his system, a system he had assured everyone was foolproof and safe.

He walked straight past the commissionaire without hearing the old man's hearty wish that he have a nice evening, turning left out of the apartment block on to the bustling street.

Darkness had begun to take its grip on the evening, and all around him artificial light blazed from aircars and from the skyscraping apartment blocks in this residential suburb of Darwin. A few metres ahead two drunks hailed a cab and stood watching as it hovered over to them, dropping on to its rubber cushions with a gentle sigh. Bradman gave them a wide berth and broke into a trot once he was past. He arrived at the teleport station hot and breathless, and his voice came in quick uneven gasps as he gave instructions to the computer which then debited his company credit chip for the cost of the journey. There were one or two other people hanging around the station, but none of them seemed to him to be the sort who could afford the luxury of teleport travel. A young couple—he put them at about 18 or 19—walked slowly ahead of him, giggling, arm in arm. And an elderly man, carrying a brown bottle and wearing a grey coat which had clearly seen better days, was ambling up the ramp towards the double doors.

Brusquely Bradman pushed past, ignoring the teenagers' abusive comments. There was no time for messing about; he was man in a hurry, a man with a mission. These people shouldn't be here, anyway, he thought. How can they afford to be beamed through a teleport?

Only one of the doors hissed aside as he strode up to it. He was used to them both opening to cope with the rush hour crowd he usually travelled with, wanting to get to Darwin's main business area on the seafront. As usual the stark, clinical whiteness of the empty interior assaulted his eyes momentarily. He thrust his credit chip into the slot for verification that he had, indeed, just given the computer the correct details.

"Station Five, and quickly," he demanded, looking through the toughened-glass panelling into the control centre beyond. "I'm in a hurry."

The operator stared back impassively. "There's a couple more people coming in. I'm sorry, but you'll have to wait for them."

Bradman cast an irritated glance over his shoulder at the teenagers and the old man as they strolled up the ramp. He pressed himself into a corner of the ten-metre teleport booth, hoping they would not try to start a conversation with him. The old man headed for the opposite corner, while the young couple stood in the centre. The girl turned to Bradman.

"This is our first time," she enthused, her eyes bright and shining. "In a teleport, I mean. What's it like?"

What *was* it like—what was the sensation of having a computer unscramble your bodily molecules at a sub-atomic level, transmit them like an email through the ether, and then reassemble them in (hopefully!) the right sequence by the computer at the destination booth? "Wait and see," muttered Bradman. "It'll be over before you know it, anyway." He looked angrily at the operator through the glass, willing him to beam them away from the city's Southern suburban sprawl to Station Five on the Northern waterfront.

At last, he thought as the operator's blue-uniformed arm reached out towards the computer keypad.

In the same second that he saw the red transmitter light engage and felt the faint vibration of the teleport booth energising, he became aware of wailing sirens and the operator's colleague yelling: "Malfunction! Don't send them."

But the slight dimming of the lights and the milkiness of the sudden empty void beyond the glass panel told Bradman it was too late; they had already been sent on their way. The siren died instantly, as did the frantic shouting from the control room. They were miles away by now.

The old man cast Bradman a wary look, but the teenagers seemed untroubled, lost in their own world of wonder, romance and awe. The two pairs of young eyes stared around, seemingly fascinated at the emptiness.

"We're stuck," announced the old man suddenly. "Trapped in the void."

"Stuck? What do you mean?" The girl's voice was getting higher with every word. She gripped her boyfriend's arm.

"It's broken down," said the old man cheerfully. "We could be here for days."

"Shut up," snapped Bradman, seeing the youngsters turn deathly pale. "We've been reassembled here, *wherever* here is. So there's nothing to really worry about. We're in one piece."

"But it's still broken down," said the old man. "We could be here for days and days." He unscrewed the top from his bottle, thrusting the neck into his mouth and taking a deep swig of its contents.

"Ah, that's better," he sighed, wiping the moisture from his lips with the back of a grubby hand. "Oops, sorry, forgetting my manners." He offered the bottle to Bradman who waved it away with a disgusted look. The old man's noble gesture elicited the same response from the teenagers.

"What did you mean when you said we could be stuck here for days?" The girl's voice was quivering, still high pitched, and Bradman guessed she was on the verge of hysteria. *For God's sake don't let her be claustrophobic*, he found himself thinking.

"Days and days and days," echoed the old man after another gulp from his bottle. He belched, and the strong, sickly scent of sweet cider reached Bradman's nostrils.

"What do you mean?" cried the girl again. Her boyfriend laid his arm protectively around her shoulders, but Bradman felt he, the boyfriend, was probably as much in need of comfort as she was.

"We're stuck here until they can mend it," said the old man.

"How long will that be?" asked the boy, his voice shaky.

"As long as it takes." The old man fastened his bottle and slipped it into the depths of his shabby, grimy overcoat. "But it could take days and days and days."

Bradman stared at the tramp's old lined face, noting with distaste the small weasel eyes set too close together, the lank grey hair desperately in need of a wash, and the narrow tapering chin desperately in need of a shave.

"Just what do mean by that?" he demanded. For all that he had used the teleport almost daily for the past 15 years to commute to his office, along with regular site visits, he had never experienced a breakdown and had no idea how long a repair was likely to take.

Suddenly he felt a great—and somewhat uncharacteristic—surge of pity for the pathetic young couple; their first exciting time being beamed across Darwin had been spoiled. They would probably never want to see the inside of a teleport booth again.

But Bradman kept the bulk of his sympathy for himself. He was having to share time with this disgusting old man. Time when he was needed urgently elsewhere.

The weasel eyes stared back at him in silence.

Bradman was beginning to lose patience. "I asked you a question," he snapped, then promptly took a pace backwards as a rumbling began somewhere in the depths of the cider-pickled stomach, working its way up to become another full-blown belch.

"What time is it?" demanded the old man, patting his stomach, post-belch.

"He wants to know the time!" A note of almost comical exasperation crept into Bradman's voice as he spread his hands helplessly towards the young couple.

"No, please," insisted the old man. "It's important."

Bradman glanced at the digital display screen on his wrist, expecting it to say somewhere between eight and nine o'clock. After all, he had only been out of the apartment about 20 minutes and Alpha-Zero was still on the 3D holo when he left.

He stared at his watch in astonishment. Eleven minutes past four! *It can't be.* He glanced up, a frown creasing his brow. Another look. The same. And he noted that the seconds had stopped, too.

"It's stopped. What have you done to my watch?" he shouted angrily.

Before the old man could respond, the boy chipped in: "Mine's stopped, too. But this can't be right, it says four-eleven."

The girl turned her puzzled face towards Bradman. "And mine."

Bradman was beginning to feel out of his depth. All three watches were showing the same time. The same *wrong* time: four-eleven and fifteen seconds. The old man appeared to be doing a calculation in his head, silently mouthing figures while counting off the fingers on his left hand. He raised an arm as Bradman started to speak. "No. Quiet," he ordered. There was a new degree of authority to his voice.

Like a tame lamb Bradman stood mute, waiting obediently for him to finish.

"Right," said the old man eventually. "Sorry about that. Just working something out, you know."

Bradman just had to ask. "What?"

"You were expecting it to be about half past eight, weren't you?" He didn't seem to notice Bradman's limp nod of acknowledgement, but carried straight on. "Your watches say just after four... yes? A difference of four and a half hours, right? So, any time now...." He broke off, extending both arms towards the doors.

Nothing.

"Well?" Bradman asked after a couple of moments.

The old man frowned. "My timing can't be that much out, surely. Ah, here we are."

As he spoke the double doors hissed aside to let daylight flood it. *Daylight.* Bradman thought for a fleeting second that he must be going mad. It had been getting dark outside when they stepped into the teleport. And what were all those people doing outside, just standing there, stock still like statues? Dozens of people, completely immobile.

"Come on, I've got something to show you." The old man sounded like an excited schoolboy. Bradman didn't protest when he felt his arm being gripped, but simply trotted alongside with the young couple bringing up the rear.

All around them the city lay in eerie stillness. Except the city wasn't Darwin. Bradman recognised it thanks to the times he had emerged from the teleport on his visits to the Macdonnell Conversion Plant. This was Alice Springs. The busy main street was full of aircars, but they were all frozen in mid-movement, and not a sound reached Bradman's ears apart from their four sets of footsteps.

"What's happened?" he managed to stammer. "It's almost as if... well... as if time's standing still for everyone except us."

The old man rubbed his hands together gleefully. "I'm proud of you, Mr Bradman, I truly am." Bradman didn't begin to wonder how the old man knew his name. In fact, he did not even notice having been addressed by name, he was too engrossed in wondering about other things. "That's exactly what's happened, Mr Bradman, the malfunction in the teleport has caused us to remain 'in transit' so to speak, trapped between two stations. At that moment in time we were physically nothing more than particles of concentrated molecules, but we had to materialise somewhere. The calculation as to where, is based on the speed we were being transmitted and the distance we were travelling."

Bradman stared at the impossibly frozen world around them. "But this isn't Darwin, it's Alice Springs."

"I don't expect even a world-renowned physicist like yourself to understand the temporal science behind this." The old man sounded somewhat smug, rather like an unpopular lecturer explaining something to a none-too-bright student. "All you need know is that we've flipped backwards to a frozen moment in time shortly after four o'clock this afternoon in Alice Springs."

It was impossible for Bradman to rationalise what he was hearing. "Gone back in time?" he sneered. "Don't talk nonsense. What's really happened to us?"

The old man chuckled to himself. "They never believe it, never. I don't know why I bother to explain."

The young couple were staring up at the sky. Thousands of metres above them a hyperboosted aircraft simply hung in the deep blue.

"You believe me, don't you?" he asked them.

They turned towards him, blank expressions masking their faces.

"Never mind," he said briskly. "It's Mr Bradman I'm concerned with."

Bradman, too, looked at him blankly. "What have you done to us?"

"What have I done to you...?" The rhetoric was slow and patient—again like lecturer to student. "I've given you a unique opportunity, Mr Bradman, that's what I've done to you. I've given you a chance to live a few short hours of your life again, to put matters right. Do you follow me now?"

Suddenly, like a flash of lightning, Bradman was able to grasp the old man's meaning. "I don't know how or why, but, yes, I think I do. I can stop the malfunction at the Macdonnell Conversion Plant."

"Absolutely, Mr Bradman." The weasel eyes shone. "You're a worthwhile pupil indeed. I'm proud to be your mentor."

"How much time do I have?"

"Until they can figure out what we've done to the teleport."

"How long do you think that'll be?"

"Well, I hope not until you've completed your task."

"But the plant's miles away, in the Macdonnell mountain range."

"Your transport awaits you, Sir."

Bradman's eyes followed the old man's outstretched arm, coming to rest on a cab frozen at the roadside. Its door was open and two women had been stopped in time just as they were alighting. The old man gently lifted them out of the way and climbed inside. He slid the equally motionless driver across the seat, then deftly flicked his fingers over the computer console.

"Come on, Mr Bradman, get in."

As Bradman scrambled into the back he heard the door hiss shut and the engine power up.

"Hey, what about us?" cried the teenage boy from outside, knocking on the window.

"Don't worry," called the old man. "We'll pick you up on the way back."

Bradman peered out at them as the car rose, before shooting away westwards towards the outback and the still intact Macdonnell mountain range.

* * *

The teenagers stared at the aircar until it was nothing more than a tiny dot in the distance, and absolute stillness descended to their world once more.

"Well, I like that," snapped the girl. "What do we do now?"

Her boyfriend gazed around at the surreal sight of Alice Springs frozen in time, the frozen people, the frozen cars, the frozen aircraft. "It's like a photograph. A 3D holograph which we're walking through."

"We'd better not go too far from here," the girl continued. "We don't want to miss our ride home."

Suddenly the boy caught a glimpse of movement out of the corner of his eye. "Hey, there's someone over there."

Before his girlfriend could react he sprinted 20 metres to a narrow alleyway. Three tramps wearing similar filthy coats to the one adorning the old man who had taken them there, sat leaning against the wall, apparently frozen in time like everyone and everything else. But a fourth tramp was shuffling his way down the alley.

"Wait a minute," shouted the boy as the shambling figure veered drunkenly to one side and vanished through a door.

The boy was halfway down the alley when he heard a scream from behind him. "Tony. Help me!" He whirled round and saw his girlfriend struggling with the other three tramps. Her arms were held firmly while one tramp swiftly injected her in the neck with a power-boosted syringe. She went limp, and the three men gently laid her on the ground.

"Saralee!" yelled Tony, running back towards them. "What have you done to Saralee?"

The tramps formed a line between Tony and the girl, but that did not stop him. Without breaking stride he flung himself straight at them. Two went down with him, but the third managed to squeeze against the wall to avoid the human battering ram.

For all that Tony was young and fit he did not stand a chance against all three. Because they were not as derelict as they looked. They seemed to shake off the appearance of stooped, drunken losers in an instant, becoming lithe and strong. In a few seconds they had overpowered him, and one reached nimbly inside his stained and tattered coat for another power-boosted syringe.

"Who are you?" screamed Tony, struggling fiercely, trying to break away from the conquering grip which held him firm. "What are you doing to us?"

The tramp's voice sounded surprisingly young and vibrant. "Don't struggle," he ordered smoothly. "We're not going to hurt you. We're taking you home, that's all."

"Home... but how?" Tony's eyes widened in fear as the syringe hovered perilously close to his neck. The tramp holding it thrust his face close to Tony's. "When you wake up you'll be in the teleport booth and you won't remember a thing about this." He pressed the syringe into Tony's flesh and fired the trigger.

In the second or two before losing consciousness Tony caught a glimpse of the fourth tramp coming back up the alley, pulling off his coat to reveal a dark blue uniform beneath. It was the teleport operator, whom he had last seen in the Darwin control chamber. The man almost swam across his fading vision.

"Hurry up," Tony heard him say, the words sounding faint as his senses reeled. "I'm ready to get...."

Then Tony sank into oblivion.

* * *

Bradman stared through the aircar's window at the town lying silent and still as they sped towards the urban boundary and the wilderness beyond: the outback, where the Macdonnell Conversion Plant lay in the heart of the mountain range.

He could scarcely believe what was happening. "Just who are you," he ventured to ask. "How are you doing all this?"

The old man eased the joystick to manoeuvre the car round a vehicle in front of them suspended both in the air and in time. He glanced back over his shoulder at Bradman sitting in the rear.

"Let's just say I'm utilising forces of nature which you haven't learned to tap yet."

"But who are you?"

"Enjoy the trip, Mr Bradman."

"But what…?"

"If I were you I'd start thinking how to rectify that malfunction in your reactor." The old man gestured at the statuesque landscape beyond the aircar's windshield. "It may look like it out there, but you haven't really got all the time in the world. You'll have to work fast." He hit a key on the console and a sound-proof sheet of plastiglass slid up smoothly between them, cutting him off from any more questions.

Bradman nestled back in his seat and began to picture the reactor's main circuit board.

But try as he might, concentration continued to elude him. His mind was still reeling from the considerably unlikely events of the day. First, the explosion caused by a malfunction—more likely two malfunctions—in the system he told everyone was failsafe; in fact, the number of safety features built into it had become legendary amongst his fellow Datateknik directors who felt he was being too cautious. Secondly, what was happening to him now totally defied belief. For a moment or two he seriously considered the possibility that he might be dreaming—that this was all a nightmare. But he could clearly recall all he had done during the day; what he ate for lunch and dinner, the appointment he had kept and the people he had seen. And just before leaving the office he had made his final commitment to Walter Redbrick that the result of a full month's on-line test operation of the prototype reactor, following its successful month's offline simulation, would be ready within two days. No, he had definitely not been dreaming that. So had he fallen asleep watching Alpha-Zero? He was confident he had not. He stared hard through the plastiglass at the back of the old man's head, noting how the straggly grey hair hung in greasy strands over his collar.

Again he looked outside. The sprawl of civilisation thinned as the aircar raced towards the south-western border of Alice Springs. Within moments they were flying over the desolate brush-land, the spread of buildings behind them no more than shrinking dots on the horizon.

Eventually they reached the outer rim of the Macdonnell range, where the inhospitable flat terrain began to bulge into hills and mountains. Bradman had made this trip many times, but none in such bizarre circumstances. It still defied belief that beyond the confines of the aircar the whole world was apparently frozen in time, and that he was on his way to prevent a cataclysmic explosion that had already happened. But no, it *hadn't* happened, had it? Not yet? At least not in this particular moment in time, four hours into his past. And yet, in his own present it had. Forcing those inexplicable paradoxes to the back of his mind he summoned every ounce of willpower he had to bring his thoughts under control. The reactor. What caused the reactor to break down, and why did the monitoring system not alert the operators? A self-diagnostic run on the computer would be the quickest way of pinpointing what needs to be done, he thought. But even that will take some time. Are there any other ways of doing it?

Under the expert control of the elderly tramp the aircar wound its way unerringly between the base of several mountains until it came to Solar Peak—the unofficial name afforded it by the Datateknik team working inside and hundreds of metres underground. The vehicle climbed to a flat ledge about 100 metres up, then sank onto its cushioned supports with a hydraulic hiss. The old man touched two buttons to open the front and rear doors, and climbed out.

Bradman alighted, too. His companion pointed to a small slot in the rock face. "I believe I need you for this," he said amiably. Alongside the slot, it was almost as if a giant knife had scored a mathematically perfect three-metre square in the face of the mountain.

"Yes." Bradman's voice positively dripped sarcasm. "I'll open the door for you." For a second or two he stood looking out across the desolate landscape. Nothing moved. Indeed, there was nothing there *to* move.

The tramp pulled up a sleeve and made an exaggerated show of looking at his watch. There was something about that simple action that rang warning bells for Bradman, but for the life of him he could not put his finger on it.

"Mr Bradman, please...." It seemed the old man was becoming increasingly worried about rectifying the problem in time.

"Are you able to help me find the fault?" asked Bradman. "I could do with some assistance once we get inside. It'll be quicker if we're both working on it."

The old man shook his head. "Regrettably not. If I could, I wouldn't need to bring you here, would I? I would do it myself, but sadly I don't have enough working knowledge of your process. You're the expert, and I'm told you're the only one who can possibly carry this off."

Bradman cast him a cynical glance before pushing his company ID chip into the slot. Immediately a small horizontal section of rock, roughly the size of Bradman's i-tablet, extended out from the rock face to reveal an opaque scanning screen. Bradman then pressed the palm of his right hand on to it, activating the computer's voice circuits.

"Access time: four-eleven and 15 seconds, July 30th, year 2345." The computer had been programmed with a soft female voice of neutral accent. "Personnel: Bradman, Lloyd Timothy Michael. Status: Datateknik Energy Director. Handprint verified. Access granted."

With a gentle electronic buzz, the three-metre square slid smoothly aside, revealing a stark white corridor illuminated by concealed ceiling lights.

Once they were inside the door hissed shut, and the only sound was the hollow tap of their footsteps on the metallic floor as Bradman led the way to an elevator door. "Down to the 87th level," he said, gesturing for the old man to go through.

Bradman was hoping there would be enough time for the control computer to run its full self-diagnostic program, when the old man's question cut in on his thoughts. "I'm told your energy conversion process is a spectacular concept. How did you come across it?"

Bradman loved talking about his favourite subject—particularly his role in devising the current experimental reactor system—but he could only speak of it in the right circles. One of the reasons the project was tucked away deep underground and in the heart of a mountain in the Australian Outback, was that it was still very much at the classified stage. Only a handful of very senior government officials were aware of its existence. And Bradman knew that when it became public knowledge there would be a vociferous protest from the solar and hydrogen power industries. But, of course, if his mission in preventing the coming tragedy should fail, the whole world would know about it in a matter of hours, which would spell the end for Datateknik's revolutionary solar wind conversion scheme. And this unsavoury man *was* helping him, so what harm could it do to skirt around the edges a little?

He glanced at the floor-indicator. Just a few seconds more to the 87th.

"Well, what we do is to convert the solar wind into a form of almost limitless power," he began.

"I thought we already had that resource, Mr Bradman."

"I beg your pardon?"

"We've been using solar cells to convert sunlight directly into electricity for 300 years. What's so special about your process?"

"*Sunlight*, yes. That's been powering many homes and businesses for centuries through individual semi-conductors, and most satellites currently orbiting the Earth draw on sunlight for their power. The raw energy the Earth gets from the sun is mainly light and various forms of electromagnetic radiation which is used to generate heat or electricity. But the particular type of solar cell needed to utilise it is still too inefficient and expensive to be used on a global scale, commercially.

"The solar wind, however, is a totally different matter."

Almost imperceptibly the elevator ended its descent to level 87, many thousands of metres underground. The door sighed open and Bradman stepped out, indicating that they should turn right.

"A stream of charged particles originates in the sun's corona, and is ejected from the upper atmosphere," he continued. "But this wind is highly unstable. Direction and speed vary considerably, and quite often high speed winds hit those travelling slower. These wind speed variations buffet the Earth's magnetic field and can produce storms in our magnetosphere."

"Magnetosphere?"

"The magnetosphere acts as a barrier, deflecting the particles around the Earth. However, sometimes they're able to penetrate the edge of this region, and can cause radio interference. Occasionally these storms are so severe that they knock out our power grids."

"Is that what caused the worldwide power outage in 2310?"

"Absolutely, and the one that hit Australia in 2335, along with numerous others over the years. But if the solar wind's properly harnessed it can be used on a commercial basis to power the entire world.

"Our project is geared towards channelling and taming the solar wind. We have a number of channelling dishes at the top of this mountain to collect that energy and drop it into a series of underground reactors...."

"Where you convert it into the cheapest form of power Mankind has ever had," concluded the tramp. "But what about the cost to the environment? What harm is it doing to the Earth?"

"Absolutely none. As well as being the cheapest, it's also the safest, cleanest and greenest form of energy. Unlimited cheap energy for as long as we want it."

"Are you absolutely sure of that? They had the same high hopes for nuclear energy in the mid 20th Century. Was it not confidently predicted that nuclear power would usher in a golden age for humanity—the cost of energy would be too cheap to even bother monitoring?"

He had obviously read his history files, mused Bradman.

"But what actually happened?" An unpleasant sneer fixed itself on the tramp's face, his eyes holding Bradman's unwaveringly. "There were many accidents involving nuclear meltdown, were there not? You've had your first major accident already and you're not even operational yet."

"Yes, I know. But thanks to your help—however you're doing this—we can correct that fault and ensure it doesn't happen again," said Bradman. "Ah, here we are." They had come to a door at the end of the corridor, which gently slid aside, revealing the reactors' normally highly guarded control area. The personnel on the day shift were all eerily immobile at their stations, and again Bradman found himself wondering how the malfunction, whatever it was, had failed to be picked up.

He eased a frozen scientist away from his post at the telemetry monitor and sat down, hitting the key to return the computer to its start-up screen. Using a combination of the keyboard's touchpad and the on-screen icons he flicked through the launch sequence for the main reactor's systems diagnostic, noting with a sinking feeling that the full run would take around 40 minutes.

Hovering menacingly in the background, the old man was checking his watch, becoming agitated. A fleeting thought flashed through Bradman's mind that back in the teleport booth the tramp had asked him the time. And that was what had gnawed away at him when they stood on the entrance ledge earlier. *Why would he ask me the time when he's got a watch himself?* The thought dissipated as he returned his attention to the computer.

The diagnostic unearthed a few minor systems errors which it repaired automatically, but the minutes specially given by this enigmatic figure outside the normal flow of time, ticked away ... until:

"Here it is," cried Bradman, pointing to the computer screen and pausing the diagnostic scan. "A cracked control rod."

Then his face fell. "We don't keep any replacements on site. We've never had a problem with the rods before. I'll have to go back to Darwin to get a new one."

Again there was a glance at the watch, and the tramp shook his head. "No, Mr Bradman, you're asking too much now. You don't have time to replace it."

"Then why the hell did you bring me here?" shouted Bradman. "I thought I was coming to fix the problem, to prevent the explosion." He sank back into the seat, defeated. "If I can't replace the rod I can't stop the disaster."

"But you can."

"I *can't.* Don't you understand? This rod is what caused the chain reaction. It's cracked and I can't mend it. I must replace it."

"Not necessarily." The tramp reached into the seemingly endless depths of his overcoat to retrieve the sweet cider. "Is there no other way to stop the reactors reaching a critical overload?" he asked, taking a generous swig, swallowing deeply and savouring the liquid.

"No, of course not." Suddenly realisation dawned. "Except…the warning system."

The tramp secreted the bottle away in the folds of his coat once again. As before, after emerging from the teleport booth, he rubbed his hands gleefully and a patronising tone entered his voice. "Of course, Mr Bradman. I am truly proud to be your mentor. What you must do is ensure that the warning system's functioning properly, make the operators realise something's wrong. If they know that, they can prevent the explosions, can't they?"

Bradman's eyes gleamed. "Yes, indeed, and there shouldn't be a problem with that, either. If the circuit's faulty there are plenty more here which I can put in. We do keep those on site." He unclipped a panel in the processing motherboard and removed the central warning core, examining it carefully.

"No sign of any wear or loose circuit wires," he said.

"It must malfunction sometime in the next hour, though," said the tramp. "Get the new one in quickly, before the teleport's fixed and we're whisked out of this time bubble back to your own present."

"Right. The new ones are over here." Bradman started to hurry towards a storage area, but again found his arm in a vice-like grip.

"Just a moment, Mr Bradman. Is the computer now completely blind to the malfunction in the reactor?"

"It is, yes." As he spoke, Bradman caught for the first time the evil glint in the weasel eyes and saw, too late, the old man's other hand raised high above his head, before smashing the now empty cider bottle with alarming force on to his exposed temple. As the glass shattered around his ear and fell in fragments, Bradman saw stars before crumpling senseless to the floor.

Standing over him the old man looked down at the jagged stump of the bottle still in his hand. "The old-fashioned ways are always the best," he said. "Just as effective as these new-fangled booster syringes."

* * *

Bradman winced as the medic rubbed ointment into the bruise. "I just don't understand it, Walter."

"Don't worry about it, Lloyd. At least you're okay, although you've got a nasty bruise on your head. You must have been jolted pretty hard against the wall when you finally materialised."

Since recovering consciousness several moments ago Bradman had been trying to get things clear as to what had happened. "How long were we trapped in limbo?" he asked, a little uncertainly.

"Almost three hours," replied Redbrick.

Long enough to have travelled to Macdonnell and disconnected that warning circuit, Bradman thought miserably. Suddenly his addled brain began to see things in a clearer light. "The old man. What's happened to the old man?"

A puzzled look creased Redbrick's brow and played at the corners of his mouth. "What old man?"

Now it was Bradman's turn for puzzlement. "The old man in the teleport."

Rebrick shook his head. "There wasn't any old man, Lloyd. Just you and two teenagers."

The words stunned Bradman and his head refused to stop spinning. Okay, so his brain was still addled, but not *that* addled. No old man? It did not make any sense. "But he was in there with us," he protested.

Redbrick laid an arm on his shoulder. "Don't worry, Lloyd. It's the bang on the temple that's done it."

"But those teenagers saw him, too. They came to Alice Springs with us."

Redbrick shrugged his shoulders. "We've already spoken to them. They didn't mention any old man—they said there was just you in the teleport with them. And Lloyd, you didn't go to Alice Springs. You materialised in Station Five on the waterfront at Darwin."

Bradman's mind continued its dizzying whirls. "But the old man... what could have happened to him?" *If he was really there at all.* This from an inner voice which hardly sounded convincing.

"We've spoken to the teleport operator as well." Walter Redbrick's words were as gentle and as soothing as he could make them. "He told us there were just three of you on that trip."

"But the old man was there in the teleport, too," insisted Bradman. "He *was*. He took me on to Macdonnell and...." He broke off in a cold sweat as a terrible thought crossed his mind. "Oh God, no," he gasped, looking at Redbrick in anguish. Brushing the medic's arm aside he pushed himself up on to his elbows. You told me on the vidlink that the telemetry readout pinpointed the exact time of the reactor's malfunction...?"

Redbrick nodded. "That's right, Lloyd. It seems the main control rod cracked around quarter to four, but there wouldn't have been enough build-up in the other reactors to trigger the warning system until much later. Unfortunately the circuit controlling the warning system malfunctioned as well."

Bradman felt faint and sick. "What time did the safety circuit go offline?" His voice was distant and helpless. He knew the answer already.

"About ten past four, I think."

It had to be more accurate than that. He could still hear the teenage boy saying his watch had stopped at four-eleven, and his own incredulity on realising that everyone's watches had stopped at that same wrong time. It was also the time the computer logged his access to the Macdonnell site.

"Do you have the exact minute and seconds?"

Redbrick looked puzzled again. He pulled up a file on his i-tablet. "Yes, here we are. Four-eleven and fifteen seconds."

Ashday's Child

With each passing week the ritual grew more poignant and he dreaded the prospect of walking across the plain to the towering stone pillars of the mighty henge.

And when the Holy Man and Star-Gazer extended their arms heavenward to praise the All-Seeing-All-Powerful-One for the coming of another seven dawns, he felt every eye was on him, knowing of his sin.

Yet how could they know? The secret lay buried deep in his own heart, shared only with Laoni. But he kept asking himself how long it would be before her body began to swell as the child within her grew, exposing their guilt to the village.

It was not the result of deliberate defiance, just one moment of rashness, but he knew the Elders wouldn't see it that way. Laoni knew, too – the wild-eyed look of terror on his partner's face when she confessed would haunt him forever.

That was when his nightmare started.

* * *

The sun had been powerful all day, and during the last couple of hours Jontil's thoughts turned with eager anticipation to a jug or two of the strong ale which Laoni was so good at brewing. When the beasts were taken care of for the day he began the short walk home through the sloping strip of woodland separating his three acres from the village.

As he passed the last Sycamore the countryside opened up before him, rolling away to its distant rendezvous with the evening sky. He looked down upon the scores of huts scattered along the river bank; the thread of water trailing through the foot of the valley as far as the eye could see.

Laoni had promised him the tender white meat of a fatted young calf for his supper, and the twist of greyish-black smoke worming its way through the roof of his hut told him the food was already cooking over a charcoal fire. Many other huts gave off smoke, too – he would not be the only one feasting on good cooked meat that night.

He sensed something was wrong as soon as he flipped aside the lengths of hanging beads and stepped into the cool, darkened interior of his home.

"Laoni, why've you got the windows covered? There's still daylight outside."

Instead of answering, she continued to squat by the fire with her back to him, gently prodding the spit-roasting meat. Normally she would run to him, her bare feet slapping against the earthen floor, and throw herself into his arms.

"Laoni?" he called again, staring at the back of her knee-length light brown tunic and noticing her shoulders trembling slightly. There was also a tremor running through the sleek raven-black hair, as if she were rapidly nodding her head. Then he could see that her whole body was wracked with sobs.

As he hurried towards her she suddenly stood up and spun to face him. Red rings surrounded the dark brown eyes and her breath came in rough, uneven gasps as he clasped her to his chest, stroking her hair soothingly.

"Come on," he whispered. "What is it? What's wrong?"

She eased herself away from his grip and ran to the beading, peering out into the fading daylight. Then she turned back to him and led the way through the arch into the more comfortable living area of the hut. That, too, was in semi-darkness; she had draped a blanket over the window in there, as well.

He stood in silence, waiting for her to tell him what was troubling her.

"Oh, Jontil," she eventually managed to murmur between sobs. "Whatever's going to become of us?"

"What's wrong?" he repeated, smiling into her eyes to try and reassure her that whatever it was they would face it together.

She looked up at him with a haunted, fear-ridden face, and shook her head slowly. It was almost as if the words were fighting to come, but she was desperately trying to suppress them.

"I've been meaning to tell you..." she began, then stopped, turning to stare blankly at the wall.

An eternity seemed to pass before Jontil reluctantly accepted he would have to prompt her. He put his hand beneath her quivering chin and gently eased her towards him again.

"Tell me what, Darling?"

"It just never seemed to be the right moment. I was always so frightened. I'm scared, Jontil, so scared."

His heart grieved to see her this upset. While his fingers softly caressed her long dark hair his frown deepened as he tried to imagine what could be troubling her so much.

"Tell me, Laoni," he said, gently. "Please tell me what it is. I can't help you unless I know."

She took a deep breath, holding it in her lungs for longer than was comfortable, causing a red flush to race up her cheeks. When she did eventually manage to speak, the words cascaded out in a mad jumbled rush.

"Jontil, please don't be cross with me, I love you so much. I'd never do anything to hurt you or put you in danger. You know that, don't you? I'll go away or kill myself, then no-one'll ever know. Oh, what am I going to do? What...?"

"Hey, steady on. Come on, now, slow down and tell me what it is." There was something about the unusual blackness of her mood and the uncharacteristic hysteria which emitted a grim, foreboding aura.

Jontil started to pull her face towards his chest, but she broke away, taking a couple of steps backwards.

Again a deep breath; then finally it was out: "Jontil, I'm going to have a baby, *we're* going to have a baby."

Something nagged at the back of his mind, but his thoughts were instantly filled with what he imagined to be the usual euphoria of a would-be father, and he started to laugh.

"A baby!" he cried. "But that's wonderful. Why all the tears? Why the worry? Didn't you think I'd be pleased? I'm so happy, it's wonderful news."

She clasped a hand over his mouth. "Ssshhhh. Quiet!" Her voice was low, demanding, insistent.

But again Jontil laughed as he softly prised her fingers away from his face. "I don't understand what's worrying you." His mind whirled in a plethora of happy, wondrous thoughts. He was going to be a father.

Her soft, delicate features were stained by tiny rivulets of tears, and she shook her head urgently, her face a mixture of fear and frustration.

"Jontil, *think*. I'm just over a Quarter Year pregnant. The baby'll be born in the forbidden Second Quarter of the New Year. We're going to have an Ashday's Child."

That simple phrase slammed into him with all the force of a wooden club. A few seconds of numbness rooted him to the spot, giving her a chance to wrap her arms around his shoulders and cling tightly to him.

He pushed her away as if she were suddenly as hot as fire. "Oh my God. The Second Quarter. An *Ashday's Child*. Are you sure?" His momentary happiness at the prospect of becoming a father evaporated in a horrifying split second.

Laoni took a couple of paces away from him, looking small and vulnerable, her head drooping.

"I'm sure," she said. "I've been sure for weeks. We'll bring disgrace to the village." Her voice was rising all the time, verging on the borders of hysteria. "It'll be…"

"Okay, okay." Jontil pulled her towards him again before the significance of what she had just said suddenly hit him. He spun her sideways, staring hard at her stomach, looking for signs of the child. There was nothing tangible apart from some recent stitching at the side of her tunic, suggesting she may have let it out a little.

"If you've known for weeks why didn't you tell me; give me time to work something out?" he demanded.

"Don't worry," she said, smiling through the tears, seeming to regain a little more composure now her secret was out. "If I'm careful it doesn't show yet."

Jontil stared at the ceiling, his mind running away with itself, his thoughts tumbling over each other.

"Why didn't you tell me before?" he asked again. "You must stay indoors and I'll say you're ill."

Suddenly he gripped her shoulders and shook her hard. "Don't you understand what this means? They'll execute us. What we've done is blasphemy, a sin against the All-Seeing-All-Powerful-One. We've sinned against God." Now it was his turn to edge towards hysteria.

He closed his eyes, remembering when the village had been awakened by the Destroyers of Evil thundering out of the night on horseback to descend on the home of their friends Brantis and Leila, whisking them away to the henge. The following day an expectant buzz had pervaded the air during their trek to the weekly thanksgiving. Brantis and Leila had been brought out and thrust before the massed gathering. The Star-Gazer was almost consumed with fury during his hellfire sermon about breaking the golden rule of their civilisation; conceiving a child which, if allowed to be born, would enter the world during the forbidden Second Quarter; an *Ashday's Child*.

Jontil shuddered as he recalled how his voice had raised against his friends; how it was filled with hate and righteousness when he joined the chanted demands that they be stoned to death in accordance with the ancient laws. The Holy Man commanded a degree of calm as he began the ancient stoning ceremony by reminding the gathering of the sin Brantis and Leila had committed.

The Holy Man's arms raised heavenward and his voice was strong with the words that were only summoned for the cleansing ritual: "It all began long, long ago, in the days before the world died; in the days before the All-Seeing-All-Powerful-One rebuilt the world by His own magic. Before the Great Fire fanned by the Winds of Destruction blighted our land. Our realm was not as you see it today. Mankind died by his own hand, by his own ingenuity. The world was full of mechanised monsters, of great metal birds capable of taking Man in their hollow bellies from one land to another.

"Evil and wickedness controlled men's lives everywhere. There were many false star-gazers, each claiming to be able to read messages from the heavens; such as our own – the only true – Star-Gazer does today. Our true Star-Gazer succeeds because He draws His power from the All-Seeing-All-Powerful-One. Those charlatans of ancient time did not; their power was false and evil, in defiance of the Holy Orders of the day.

"After the wickedness of the Earth was consumed in fire, and our civilisation of today eventually rose from the ashes, the All-Seeing-All-Powerful-One decreed that such carnage would never return to the Earth. He blessed the family of the Star-Gazer with hereditary power to truly read the signs of the heavens, so Mankind would be warned through all eternity of that which was yet to come. That awesome and terrible power has spanned the generations to our Star-Gazer of today, who continues the tradition begun by His forefathers.

"His power, guided by the All-Seeing-All-Powerful-One, has shown the downfall of our former brother Brantis and our former sister Leila. By conceiving a child whose birth would fall within the forbidden Second Quarter – the deadly quarter when ash fell upon the Earth from the Great Fire, fanned by the Winds of Destruction – they have sinned against us all!"

His voice raised in a rallying cry. "Do you want an Ashday's Child in your midst?"

As one voice, the massed gathering had thundered back: "No!"

"Do you want a child tainted by the Mark Of Ash?"

"No!"

"Ashday – the time that the ash fell – is a time of evil and wickedness in our history, brought upon our lands by the sins of our forebears from the Old World. Do we want reminders of those dark days?"

Back came the ritualistic response: "No reminders, no Ashday's Child."

Again Jontil shuddered, this time at the memory of how he had been there casting one of the first stones at his friends' helplessly bound bodies, and how he had been amongst those laying burning torches to their hut razing it to the ground.

* * *

As the days wore on and turned into weeks he fancied he heard others whispering and casting furtive glances his way, no doubt wondering why Laoni had started keeping herself out of sight. Ever since Laoni told him they were expecting an Ashday's Child he had pondered that unless they could successfully hide her for the next two quarters they would face the same fate as Brantis and Leila.

And when the baby was born, what then? They would have to hide their offspring, too. Perhaps even kill it. After all, was it not said that Ashday's Children were tainted with the Mark of Ash – an unwelcome reminder of Mankind's ultimate folly, of that time, millennia ago, when their forefathers had caused the deadly ash to descend upon the Earth, destroying every civilisation across the globe? That story had been passed through countless generations.

How much longer could they successfully hide their guilt, he wondered... *how much longer?*

* * *

Darkness was fast ending its vigil over the countryside when Jontil joined the throng of men, women, children and babes in arms, on their way to the weekly dawn thanksgiving. He saw with dismay that Mastron, another golden-haired one, was heading towards him. There was no escape; he was too close to the henge to deviate from his path. Within seconds Mastron was alongside, matching him stride for stride. Then came the expected question: "Laoni not with you again this morning, Jontil?"

"Does it look like it?" he snapped back, keeping his head low to avoid the probing blue eyes.

Mastron laughed easily and cheerily at the indignant outburst, holding up his hands in mock surrender.

"Okay, okay, we're only concerned because we haven't seen her for a while."

Jontil glanced around cautiously to see whether anyone else was listening, but they were all too deep in their own conversations to take any notice.

"Sorry." He adopted what he hoped was a lighter tone. "It's just that she's still not well. She's a little sick and has the pain of fire around her heart." That last part was true, at least. The sickness of a morning would have kept her confined to their hut even if their unborn child were not casting a shadow of shame.

"I see," mused Mastron. But Jontil wondered whether he really did. "Tell her from me to get well soon." And with that, Mastron sprinted off to join a group of five friends who were laughing amongst themselves as they trekked through the outer pillars of the henge towards the hallowed ground beyond.

As usual, the crudely-constructed wooden stage on the far side of the arena was bedecked with offerings of fruit, vegetables and salted meat. Today it was the turn of those who had lived between 40 and 50 summers to bring gifts. Next week the honour would fall to villagers who had not yet seen 21 summers, and Jontil had already put aside a salted loin of cattle to take.

He looked around at the throng of people stretching away across the arena, everyone wearing the same type of light brown shapeless tunic, some barefoot, others with sandals strapped to the knee. And as if that drab costume were not enough of a uniform, almost everyone's hair was raven-black, tumbling in thick, cascading waves to their shoulders, male and female alike. Dotted amongst the noisy, writhing sea, however, was the occasional island of blond hair, such as Mastron's and his, Jontil's.

The sun had been above the horizon for several moments already. Its rays were slanting brightly into the henge between the enormous stone pillars, creeping towards the ancient four-branched candlestick. At the exact second the light struck it, the stage-drapes swished aside, their intricately threaded beads clattering against each other, revealing the Star-Gazer and the Holy Man in their full bejewelled glory. The sunlight, ever-strengthening inside the henge, accentuated the flashes of red, gold, green, yellow and blue which zig-zagged across their white ankle-length robes. The Star-Gazer remained still while the Holy Man took four paces forward and flung his arms wide; the first fingers of each hand pointing heavenward; the remaining fingers bunched tightly into a fist.

He threw back his head, and an ear-splitting roar shot from his lips: "All-Seeing-All-Powerful-One, we give Thee thanks for the dawning of another seven days."

Jontil joined the congregation's response, his voice harsh and raucous in the rhythmic chanting: "Sunday, Sunday, we thank Thee for Sunday."

His mind raced back to Laoni at their hut, but still the words came. Like the scores of other villagers in the henge he did not need to think about his role in the weekly thanksgiving ritual. Having taken part every week for as long as he could remember, his responses were totally automatic.

"Sunday, Sunday, we thank Thee for Sunday." This time each syllable was accompanied by a matching-tempo handclap.

"Fireday, Fireday, the time that the World burned.

"Ashday, Ashday, the time that the ash fell."

The volume of the ritualistic chanting increased, as did the tempo, quickly building to a deafening crescendo.

"Sunday, Sunday, the time we saw the Sun.

"Moonday, Moonday, the time the Moon shone through."

Reaching fever pitch, the crowd, which numbered almost all of the 300 villagers, whipped into a frenzy; every head slashing the air wildly from side to side as the words tumbled from their spittle-flecked lips – Fireday, Ashday, Sunday, Moonday, representing the four quarters of their year, including that forbidden Second Quarter of Ashday.

Having arrived at its zenith the chanting died abruptly, leaving the clapping to fade away slowly. The Holy Man lowered his arms, his piercing black eyes scanning the villagers. Then he waved his hand across the food beside him.

"Dwellers of Thiecon, the All-Seeing-All-Powerful-One thanks you through me, His Chosen One, for these gifts; the fruit of your labours."

The villagers responded as one: "In return, He gives us Life."

Again the Holy Man's arms reached for the skies. "He thanks you for the fruit."

"In return He gives us Light," thundered the chorus of voices.

"He thanks you for the vegetables."

"In return He gives us Sun and Rain to bless the land."

"He thanks you for the meat."

"In return He gives us Rest."

"He thanks you for your worship."

"In return He gives us Salvation."

"Dwellers of Thiecon, your commitment and loyalty to Him, The All-Seeing-All-Powerful-One, are rewarded. He sends the Star-Gazer to guide you."

"By holy and ancient Thiecon lore He sends the Star-Gazer to guide us."

"He commands that you do the Star-Gazer's bidding."

"We will do the Star-Gazer's bidding."

The Star-Gazer stepped forward to take the Holy Man's place at the centre of the stage. His voice held none of the rich, robust qualities of the one the gathering had just heard, being more of a thin, whining cackle. From Jontil's place at the very back of the henge he had to strain to hear the words. But hear them he must. He could scarcely afford to miss what the day had in store for him.

"For those born in the First Quarter," cried the Star-Gazer, "today gives you the chance to close any outstanding bartering deals, but it won't come easily – you will need to give plenty in return for what you gain.

"Toilers of the land beware. Your downfall today will be of your own making."

Jontil gave a startled jump. That was him, a toiler of the land. The Star-Gazer had spoken, so he must be extra vigilant to make sure things did not go wrong today.

He stared hard at the Star-Gazer. Just how much did he know? How far did his powers stretch? It seemed to Jontil that the noble, hook-nosed head with its iron-grey hair held back in a pony tail, was staring almost hypnotically in his direction. Abruptly Jontil turned his face away, still feeling those jet-black eyes boring through the back of his skull.

That night, Laoni's shallow breathing on the rough sackcloth pillow by Jontil's ear told him she was asleep. He wished he could drop off so easily, but his thoughts continued to turn mercilessly to the increasingly dangerous situation they found themselves in. He wondered whether the village Elders would be able to help them…he had heard tales of herbal remedies being able to remove an unborn baby from its mother's womb for the Elders to cast into the flames of a sacred fire, so it should have no life of its own. *Maybe tomorrow I'll talk to a village Elder, see what can be done.*

Gradually his thoughts became more indistinct, as sleep began to wash over him, drenching him in a dream of villagers screaming that they knew the terrible secret he was trying to conceal.

A first the ungodly sound was just a part of his nightmare. Then he realised the baying of hounds and horses came not from inside his mind but from beyond the walls of his hut. Leaping up, he cast off the reed matting from the bed and rushed to the window, pulling aside the covering and peering out into the moonlit night.

It was a full moon, clearly showing that the Destroyers of Evil were abroad, threading their way through the huts.

"Laoni," he screamed, rushing back to the bed and shaking his wife violently. "They're coming for us...the Destroyers of Evil are coming for us. Run, quick, before it's too late."

Instantly she was awake, with raw, savage fear twisting her pert features. Clothed as they were, only in their night-robes, they fled through the main living area of the hut and out into the moonlight, now turned a fiery orange from the flaming torches held aloft by the Destroyers of Evil, who sat mighty and proud, astride their steeds, surrounding the hut.

Frantically Jontil looked for a way past them, but none was to be had; so tightly closed were their ranks.

"No," he screamed. "Leave us alone."

Heads began to appear through arches and windows. Heads with leering faces and glinting eyes. Word that the Destroyers of Evil were out must have spread like wildfire through the village.

All around, Jontil heard whispered voices getting louder all the time, starting to chant until they reached a crescendo, hypnotically repeating the same phrase over and over: "Destroy the evil, wipe it out. Seek and slay this very night."

Laoni screamed hysterically, covering her ears as if shutting out the mesmeric sound would erase its power and the threat of what she knew was sure to come.

Moonlight flashed off the wickedly sharp spears pointing down at them from the gloved hands of the masked riders, whose capes swirled around the horses' flanks. A tall, snorting stallion moved to one side, making way for a multi-colour-robed figure to step through the gap; a figure with a ribbon holding his iron-grey hair into a pony-tail. His eyes bored into Jontil's, then he turned to stare fiercely at Laoni.

"Yes," said the Star-Gazer impassively, his reedy voice straining to be heard above the wild chanting. "This is Jontil and Laoni Almana. The powers of foresight granted to my family for generations through the wisdom of the All-Seeing-All-Powerful-One do indeed show the truth, that this couple are going to spawn a child in the forbidden Second Quarter – an *Ashday's Child*."

The violent, frenzied crowd were baying ever-louder for immediate blood, even though they knew their appetites would not be satiated until tomorrow, when the Holy Man and Star-Gazer would invoke the stoning ritual as laid down by the ancient laws of Thiecon.

Four Destroyers of Evil leaped from their mounts and held Jontil and Laoni with powerful, immovable hands. Jontil frantically tried to shake them off, but to no avail. Laoni was now sobbing quietly, her hysteria burned away, almost as if she were resigned to their fate.

But not so Jontil. "You've betrayed us," he screamed insanely into the gathering crowd, writhing in a futile bid to shake himself free. "The curse of an Ashday's Child has long since been purged. You fools, don't you understand what you're doing? An Ashday's Child won't destroy you. An Ashday's Child will save you – will save the World."

His rantings were born of desperation, and he knew they were meaningless, simply a bleak attempt to escape the inevitable.

The Star-Gazer's mouth twisted into a mock semblance of a smile, and he struck Jontil viciously across the face with the flat of his gloved hand.

"You speak of betrayal." The words were so hostile, so vicious and fierce, that flecks of spittle flew from his humourless smile. "Your own actions betray you, and in turn, betray all Dwellers of Thiecon. Never again shall Mankind taint and blemish these sceptred lands."

Suddenly he tore his eyes away, pointing across the plain to the distant towering pillars, just visible in the glittering moonlight.

"Take them to the henge, to the sacrificial cell," he ordered the horsemen. Then he turned to the villagers who were crowding around the little hut.

"Come," he commanded above the din. "We have a thousand stones to find for tomorrow's ritual."

Honest Don

Don Sheppard was sweating.

His problem was unlike anything he had faced before.

He never thought he would feel like this when it came to the crunch.

Pulling his hands from his pockets, he stood motionless on the pavement outside the bank for a few moments, his mind working furiously. What on Earth was he to do?

Adrenalin pumped mercilessly into his bloodstream, making him notice how his heart was thumping uncontrollably.

It shouldn't really be a problem, he thought. After all, other people were doing it – you only had to read the crime reports in the paper to see that – so why shouldn't he?

Let's face it, although he had lost his job he still had to feed and clothe Brenda and the four children somehow. Four kids – and each one cost a fortune to look after. It seemed they were outgrowing their clothes even faster all the time.

Beads of sweat glistened on his brow, shimmering in the pale January sun. A woman, a complete stranger, hurried past, glancing into his face as she went.

He pulled his coat collar up, not for added warmth, but to cover as much of his exposed face as possible. He hoped the woman wouldn't remember him.

He glanced furtively up and down the packed High Street, at the throng of anonymous people as they scurried to and fro, in and out of shops and across the road. Living their lives.

Just like he had been, until the dreaded R word struck. Redundancy. And after ten years as a loyal worker. Hmm. Loyal. There was a word that didn't mean much nowadays. At least, not from the boss's side, he had mused when walking out of the factory on that last day.

He wondered if any of these people were looking at him. His head shot from left to right, scanning the sea of faces, searching for any he might recognise. He spotted one, too. On the other side of the road Steve Birch was just going into the same Jobcentre Plus office that he'd come out of five minutes earlier.

Don quickly turned his back and prayed that Steve hadn't seen him. He felt ashamed. But why should he be suffering pangs of guilt when he hadn't even done anything yet? Any other time he would have hailed Steve across the street. Steve had been his workmate at the factory for seven of the ten years he had been there, and they were made redundant on the same day five weeks earlier.

Now here he was, trying to stay hidden from him, skulking in the long shadows like a frightened sewer rate. Don's palms felt cold and clammy as he constantly clenched and unclenched his fists.

Should he go through with it, or not? Was it worth the risk?

He daren't tell Brenda his plan. She was so honest, she'd go spare if she knew he was even thinking of doing something like this. He knew she'd kill him, or at the very least walk out, and that was something else preying on his mind. In 14 years of marriage they had never kept any secrets from each other. So he had no option but to lie to her as well; tell her the extra money was an increase in benefit – drip it into the family coffers a little at a time.

His thoughts were interrupted as someone else he recognised came towards him. Not a friend, but an acquaintance, a man he had seen several times in The Pattern-Makers Arms. Rumour had it that the man was a detective, using the pub as a meeting place with his informer.

Now the man was coming out of the bank, slipping his wallet into his back pocket. It was too late for Don to turn away, he had been spotted.

"Mornin', Don, how's tricks?"

"Oh, alright, I suppose. Things could be better, you know how it is. Still not found anything," mumbled Don, shifting uneasily from one foot to the other.

"Well, never mind, something'll turn up."

Don nodded. "Yeah, I dare say you're right. Anyway, must press on, things to do, people to see, you know. See you."

The man disappeared into the crowd and Don breathed a sigh of relief, watching a young woman go into the bank.

His mind was made up. It had to be now or never. And he desperately needed the money. It had to be now.

He strode purposefully toward the door of the grocers next to the bank and stepped inside.

"Oh, hi, Don," said the friendly white-coated man behind the counter. "Have you come to measure up that store-room?"

"Yeah," said Don. "I've decided I will paint it for you, after all. But I must insist on cash, though. And whatever you do, don't let on to anyone. I am on benefits, you know. I'm not supposed to do any work unless I tell them."

Second Time Round

Love is always better the second time round. Or so they say – whoever *they* are.

Julie had to agree.

Oh, yes. Looking into those soulful brown eyes staring back at her, she just had to agree. Life was certainly better since Joe arrived on the scene.

Joe moved his head slightly to get more comfortable. As he closed his eyes Julie turned over on to her side and pulled the bed covers up a fraction. The central heating had gone off an hour before they came to bed and the room was feeling the effects of the wintry night outside.

But she didn't mind. Not as long as she had Joe to snuggle up to. He always kept her warm. "I love you," she whispered softly, snaking her arm around him. "You're the best thing that's ever happened to me. But you know that, don't you?"

Her relationship with Robert had been well and truly over before she ever clapped eyes on Joe – in fact, with hindsight she had no idea why she stayed with him for as long as she did. She found out about his affair while it was still in the early stages, and he had promised to break it off straight away.

"I love you," he would always say to her. "But you know that, don't you?" He could never simply utter those three little words without tagging the other six on at the end. And now, here she was, saying exactly the same thing to Joe. But she could never be absolutely sure that Joe felt the same way. It had certainly been love at first sight for her, and she just hoped Joe really did reciprocate.

Robert's journey on the straight and narrow hadn't lasted long. The thing is, he never seemed to bother hiding his tracks. The smell of perfume lingering on his collar when he dropped his shirt on the floor for Julie to pick up and wash; the smudge of lipstick on his cheek; flowers and an expensive meal on his credit card bill which she had neither received nor eaten, all gave him away.

"I love *you*, not her," he had whispered softly in her ear. "But you know that, don't you? She means nothing to me."

"Then why do it?" she screamed back at him. "Why sleep with her when I'm here at home waiting for you?"

Julie's eyes now traced the shape of Joe's sleeping body under the covers, as she thought of the windswept walk across the clifftop which they had taken that afternoon. She could almost still feel the biting wind piercing her coat, and hear the mountainous waves crashing against the coastline 50 metres below. Whatever the weather, whatever the world had to throw at her, she was all the better for being with Joe.

Robert hadn't liked it one little bit when she met Joe. Oh, it was all right for him to have affairs, but it seemed he did not like having to compete for her affections. No, Robert had shown his true colours when Joe came along, and it was only a matter of days before she threw him out. She could not stand his silent moods and the episodes of rage when he accused her of loving Joe rather than him.

Robert had been at the pub getting legless when she first snuggled up to Joe. Robert had gone wild when he came home early for a change and caught them.

"What'sh he doing here?" His slurred words had to swim through the effects of a gallon of beer.

"Robert, you're right," she said, quietly but firmly. "I love Joe, not you. I want you to leave, please."

"What are you looking at?" Robert yelled at Joe.

Joe remained silent, lying back in bed, staring at him impassively, with an almost amused expression on his face, as if he simply could not understand what all the fuss was about. He was with Julie now and that was all there was to it as far as he concerned. Robert could sling his hook straight away.

But Joe had not kept silent when Robert returned the following night – just as he and Julie were about to go to bed – pleading with her to change her mind.

"You don't need him, let him go," Robert implored her.

That was it.

Joe had had enough.

He leaped out of bed.

Robert was absolutely petrified. Joe's protests were loud enough to waken the dead. Even Julie had been a little frightened. This was a new side to Joe which she had not seen before. But deep down she was secretly more than a little pleased that he was standing up for her in this way. Especially when Robert went off with his tail between his legs, slinging his front door key on to the floor on his way out.

"I hope you'll be very happy together," he snarled sarcastically, slamming the door so hard that the whole house seemed to shake.

Julie sobbed tears of relief as she hugged Joe. Was it finally over with Robert? Could they really be happy? Just the two of them? Joe and her? She had thought so at the time, and she thought so now, looking at his sleeping form.

It had been a whole month since Robert walked out of her life. Yes, she had never been happier than she was now.

She stared at Joe for a full five minutes. Then she rubbed her hand across his body until he woke up. He looked at her with those liquid eyes, and a thumping came from under the covers as his tail lashed heavily against them. A paw emerged, which he gently laid across her hand.

Julie giggled, rolling the cocker spaniel onto his back, tickling his belly.

"I love you," she whispered into the long floppy ear. "But you know that, don't you?"

Joe's tail thumped even harder. Oh yes, he knew it, alright.

Line From The Past

The Torbay Express gathered speed as it straightened out of the bend, heading down the track towards the tunnel.

When it slipped inside, and there was nothing to see for a while, young Michael Carson turned to his grandfather with his eyes shining.

"This is great, Pops. Absolutely fabulous," he enthused. "Thanks a million."

Bob smiled at his grandson. "I'm just glad you're enjoying it." His own eyes began to take on that same sparkle which burnt in Michael's. They were so alike.

"You know, when I was your age there were trains like this all the time. Smoke pouring from the stack; those great wheels with their long coupling rods to give a better grip on the track; dirt and grime chuffing out."

"I didn't know you were that old," grinned Michael.

Bob playfully tapped his grandson's cheek. "Don't be so rude," he said with mock severity. "I'm only 74."

The smile at the corners of Bob's mouth told Michael that despite the pointing his grandfather wasn't really cross with him.

"I've always loved steam trains," said Bob, fond memories surfacing, of glorious summer days when he had set off with his own mother and father on rail journeys to the South Coast.

"What happened to them all, Pops?"

"They were replaced by diesels and electrification. Such a shame. They just don't have the character of beauties like this."

The green and brown engine emerged from the darkness of the tunnel, hauling the five Pullman coaches behind it.

"Why've we got diesels if they're not as nice as this sort?" Michael asked, a slight frown showing itself beneath his short fringe.

The sun shone brightly through the window, lighting up Michael's corn-coloured thatch, and Bob ran his fingers through the sparse remains of his own white hair as he wondered how best to satisfy the boy's natural curiosity.

"For years and years we were quite happy with these old locomotives chugging along, but then the world began to change. Gradually people wanted to get from one town to another much quicker and they started to look for ways of making the trains go faster. Men who'd always loved steam engines didn't want diesels, but in 1955 the men in charge of railways began to modernise the system. And it's gone on from there."

The furrows in the boy's brow deepened and Bob could sense his grandson puzzling over something.

"Pops..." he said eventually, as the train rattled across a set of points. "If diesels go faster, why didn't people like them?"

Bob was not unintelligent himself, but often had difficulty answering Michael's endless and pertinent questions. He knew he had a tendency to talk down to the lad, to patronise him, and yet he was aware that somehow Michael knew that to be the case. There was a keen and quick brain in Michael's head with a seemingly endless thirst for knowledge. Bob tried to picture himself at that age – 66 years ago – and wondered whether he had been the same. A long time had passed. And a lot had happened. Both to Bob and the world. Kids nowadays were so grown up, he thought. Their childhoods gone in a flash.

"Well, it's like that iPad we got you for Christmas a couple of years ago," he said. "Do you remember how you wanted a better one after six months."

"That's different, Pops. They brought out a new one which could do more things."

"Exactly. It's the same with trains. Diesels are faster and cleaner than these good old locomotives. And they're better value for money, too. Steam engines need their boilers washing out each day, their tubes swept, smokeboxes and ashpans emptied, and all the moving parts examined and cleaned. The diesels just keep going. As the needs of the world change, everything in the world has to change to meet them. Like your iPad, the steam trains became too old fashioned as time moved on.

"In those olden days people weren't used to the world changing so quickly. Locomotives had been the same for more than a hundred years. But then people wanted to go faster, they wanted the countryside to be cleaner, but they still wanted the same type of train. Scientists told them they couldn't keep things the same – things had to change, to grow, to develop. If they wanted to progress they had to make way for new things. So steam trains began to disappear and diesels took their place. Steam trains only run on private, tourist lines now."

The Torbay Express sped through a station while Michael mused over his grandfather's answer, and Bob could see the boy's attention wandering. They both glanced at the level crossing with a queue of cars stretching away on both sides of the track.

Their thoughts were interrupted by a voice from downstairs: "Come on you two, dinner's ready."

Bob ruffled his grandson's hair as he reached out to the transformer and slowed the train to a halt. "One thing doesn't change, though," he said.

"What's that, Pops?"

"Eight-year-old boys still love electric train sets. Happy birthday, Michael."

Ree – The Troll Of Dingleay

Foreword – by Gemma Sharp (fantasy novelist D. M. Cain):

The backstory to this nonsense poem is probably every bit as intriguing as the finished piece of work itself.

My friend Stewart Bint used to write a column in a local magazine, The Flyer. I read his March 14th 2014 column with particular interest. This is what he wrote:

> *Deep in the land of Dingleay,*
> *At the side of the stream where the young fish play,*
> *There lies the house of the wicked troll, Ree.*
> *Ree's house is built of sticks and stones,*
> *Tilpit twigs and puppy dog bones.*

That's as far as I could go. Fifteen years ago! And I've still got absolutely no idea what to write next.

Fortunately, that is the one and only time in my writing career that I suffered from the curse of writer's block. The weird thing is, as far as that opening stanza is concerned, my writer's block is still insurmountable.

Oh, I had a great ambition to rival Edward Lear and Lewis Carroll as a master of the nonsense poem. So I had a go. After all, people used to tell me my writing was nonsense, so why not make it proper nonsense, I thought?

I rattled off those opening five lines in very short time. Hmm, quite promising, I thought. Then I sat and looked at it. Then I sat and looked at it a bit more. Then I put it away. Then I got it out and looked at it some more. Would the next words come? Would they, heck.

Maybe I need copious amounts of wood around me to touch at this point, but the right words always seem to flow for my novels, for my football journalism, for my PR writing... even for my Flyer column! Sometimes I don't even know where my writing's going to take me, particularly in my novels where my characters, and not me, guide my fingers as they fly across the keyboard. But whether it's me or my characters in the driving seat, the words pour out like water from a tap.

I'm currently coming towards the end of the final draft and edits of my next novel "In Shadows Waiting," due for publication in early June. And where the words weren't quite right before, I don't seem to have trouble finding more suitable ones now.

But with that nonsense poem – no way. They just will not come. There's a free download of my novel Timeshaft on offer for anyone who can finish it for me.

As a primary school teacher I asked Stewart if I could use this for a class project. He readily agreed, and decided that he would use the children's work to complete his poem. Two classes, mine and my colleague, Greg Barton-Harvey's, worked tirelessly on producing their own individual poems.

Stewart was delighted with the results, and incorporated the work of over 40 children in the final version. "The standard of the children's poems and stories was absolutely staggering. I used whole verses from them, along with single lines, and individual phrases," he said.

So here it is, the finished story, written by the children of Huncote Community Primary School, Leicestershire, with a little help from Stewart Bint, who describes it as:

A poem written to be read aloud....with feeling!!

Ree – The Troll Of Dingleay

Deep in the land of Dingleay
At the side of the stream where the young fish play,
There lies the house of the wicked troll, Ree.
Ree's house is built of sticks and stones,
Tilpit twigs and puppy dog bones.

He looks like a demon, so sickeningly green
But even more horrible, sinister and mean.
Ree loves it when the snot wind blows,
His nose drippy and droopy, slurpy and slimy
Raining bogeys on hands and terrible toes.
His cackle is like a stab in the ear.
He wears rags that have never been changed.

He roams the forest all day long,
Leaving behind a gruesome pong
His monstrous feet stinking like hay
You can smell him coming a mile away.

He eats children for dinner, for lunch and a snack.
Loving to hear bones break and crack.
Under his house, there's a dungeon so deep,
Down, down, it goes,
Just like a hose.
He keeps the children chained in there.

When the sun comes out at the start of the day,
Ree lurks in the shadows, watching them play.
Someone's going to get caught today.
Watch where you step, he's not got you yet.
But when he does, into the dungeon you go.

Then when he's hungry,
With powerful jaws and terrible breath
He kills his victims – instant death:
Venomous teeth crushing life from his prey.

"Lunchtime!" the snotty troll boomed.
"Oh no!" the child screamed. "I'm doomed."
Their fate they know; just what he'll do
Is to horribly smile while he chews on you.

We saw his house, and when passing it by,
What was that smell? It was human pie!
We ran so fast out of Dingleay.
Never returning there to play.

But after we'd gone, unknown to us,
Ree changed his ways and broke the spell.
You see – a troll, he hadn't always been.
Cursed by a wizard at such a young age,
His hideous troll face was seen as a sin.

A troll; yes, he would always remain,
But his heart was not black,
And *that* is the thing.
It was love that saved Ree from his horrible fate.

One bright sunny day while hunting for berries
He slipped on some mud and fell into a stream.
Gargling and panting, he started to scream.
He roared a big roar, cursing those slippery stones.
The current was strong
    And pulled him along.

He opened his eyes and was sure he would die,
For there, up ahead, a waterfall loomed.

Down he fell, gurgling and splashing.
Then, at the *bottom* he lay, cursing and thrashing.
For the water was shallow,
He knew he would live.

Climbing out of the stream,
His heart was a'flutter.
And he ran through the woods
As if in a dream.

His thoughts were a'whirl
As he fled on and on.
When darkness descended upon that strange land
Ree started to panic – and he pleaded for someone to give him a hand.
A cottage then came into sight.
A perfect place to spend the night.

A girl troll suddenly opened the door
Ree's sweat started flooding the floor.
This girl troll was nice and invited him in,
Across Ree's face was a very wide grin.
'Cos he knew his future was about to begin.

He asked her name – she said it was Liz,
And she welcomed him in with a big sloppy kiss.
They went on a date and ate mouldy fish.
It wasn't too long before they fell in love,
And each set free a golden Dove.

Their hearts entwined,
Love reigned supreme,
And that's all from me on a tale of Ree.
Deep in the land of Dingleay,
By the side of the stream where the young trolls play.

The Dream Witch

Foreword:

Hope and reality. Are they two sides of the same coin?

Or even the same side, just viewed from a different perspective? For many people, every New Year starts with such hope and optimism. But as Father Time scythes his way through the months we all hop back on the old cycle of reality.

I've only ever written two poems in my life; Ree – The Troll Of Dingleay, and this one which has a mental health theme, looking at hope and reality, and how those two poles may actually be one and the same. It just takes a different perspective, as I hope the final line explains.

The Dream Witch

What is the point? Can anyone tell me, does anyone know?
Time's in reverse, just go with the flow.
With the sun and the moon aloft in the sky,
The reaper can't land, so off he must fly.
When attacking the weak, the strong think they are brave
While the Watcher awaits, on top of a grave.
The time is a'coming, the Cloud Master will rise
"But who will oppose the Dream Witch," he sighs.

When nightmares turn real, and dreams are forsaken
You knock on the door, hoping to waken.

When the mind is so pushed that the barriers stretch,
The unreal becomes real, then darkness falls.
The mind is so fragile and easily snapped.
So what does it take to pull back from the brink?

As winds blow on over; the lands howl out their song,
Deaf ears are hearing that everything's wrong.
The stars are ablaze, their fire so intense,
The moon is so cold, your mind makes no sense.
If people could see the damage they do,
The dead would sing, that much is true.

For when you are dead, they'll see it's too late.
The edge was too close, but that was your fate.
They pushed too hard, and over you went.
Just one last prayer bursts forth from your lips.
But the Dream Witch is here, with her hands on her hips.

Living Proof

"Come on now, don't be silly," snapped Mr G.H. Ostly as he banged the ruler five times in rapid succession on the desk. It seemed the class was testing his patience, seeing how far they could taunt their new teacher.

His words could scarcely be heard above the peals of laughter and general clamour.

Mr Ostly sighed. He knew his first day at Spookside Academy would be a little trying to say the least. But honestly, what did they take him for? He intended to show these little horrors that he was not as green as he was cabbage-looking.

Again the corner of the ruler repeatedly rapped the desk, this time with such fierceness it left tiny holes in the soft wood. "Do be quiet. I won't tell you again. If I can't hear a pin drop in this classroom in five seconds it's detention for all of you."

The laughter died at once and all 30 pairs of eyes in Class 1M glared malevolently at their new master.

One pair twinkled a little too mischievously for Mr Ostly's liking, and it came as no surprise to him when the question was asked.

"But Sir, who's to say they don't exist? You can't prove they don't?"

"The evidence is there, boy. There've been literally thousands of hunts for supernatural phenomena using quite the most sophisticated equipment in the world. Most results show a perfectly rational and reasonable explanation…"

"Most of them, Sir. Most, but not all."

"But boy, that doesn't prove there's an irrational or unreasonable explanation, does it?"

"It proves something happened that can't be explained." That brought more titters from the back of the class.

"Silence," roared Mr Ostly. He stared hard at his inquisitor. "What's your name, boy?"

"Stephen Pectre, Sir."

"Well, Stephen Pectre, let me tell you this, once and once only. What cannot be seen and what cannot be felt, doesn't exist, in my book. The supernatural is something to be found only in the pages of comic books and on the screens of moving pictures."

Pectre's hand was in the air again, the prelude to another point he wanted to make.

"But Sir...Sir...I've actually seen one. That's how I know without a doubt that they do exist."

Mr Ostly's scornful look was enough to make any lesser youngster curl up into a ball, but Pectre was not to be put off. "I was taking a short cut home, Sir, through the churchyard and I saw a figure moving up the path."

The teacher had his wish. The class was certainly quiet enough now for everyone to hear a pin drop. They waited intently for Pectre's story.

"Did the figure come out of a grave?" Mr Ostly's question positively dripped sarcasm.

"Oh, no, Sir. But it did go to a grave and put some flowers on it."

"And disappeared inside it, no doubt?"

"No, Sir. Please let me tell it as it was. I almost froze in fear when I saw it. It was coming up the path from the main gate. I'd gone into the churchyard from the side gate, joined the path at the big Yew tree and was heading down towards the main road. The figure was still some way off when I first saw it, but there was no doubt as to what it was. I leaped behind a gravestone and bobbed down, not even daring to peer out to see if it had gone.

"A good minute went by before it passed my hiding place. I still couldn't move. I just crouched there watching its back as it strode on down the path."

"Describe this figure to us."

"Yes, Sir. I didn't see its face clearly, only from a distance, you understand. But from the back it looked fairly young. It had long blonde hair and was wearing jeans and a 'T' shirt."

"Jeans and a 'T' shirt!" The exasperation in Mr Ostly's voice was plain for all to hear.

"They don't all have to be from the olden days, Sir," young Pectre insisted.

"Now look here, I've had enough of this. You're only trying to make a fool of me and it won't work."

"But, Sir...."

"I don't know why I've let it go on for so long. It stops here and now. We are the rulers of this green and beautiful land. When our time comes, whatever life force within us moves on elsewhere, to another world. In no way does any part of us stay here to haunt those left behind. Let me tell you one final time, 1M, humans are nothing but a figment of the imagination..."

"But, Sir, you've heard all the stories of humans being seen around here. Especially in the churchyard. It's not just me. Lots of us have."

"One more time, 1M. Humans are merely folklore, legend, straight out of horror stories." Mr Ostly shook his white, transparent head. "Humans really existing...ha...what piffle, what nonsense."

Young At Art

The art gallery security guard listened in amazement to the young couple's comments.

"Look at that fabulous suffusion of colour. Isn't it wonderful the way the yellow intertwines with powerful brush strokes into the green. The whole painting simply breathes life," the girl was telling her companion.

They were the third couple visiting the art exhibition within the past half hour who had seemed to find the picture fascinating. The previous couple had decided it was "stupendous," while the couple before had enthused over its technical and artistic merits.

This latest girl seemed rather more taken with the work than the boy did, describing the none-too-delicate swirling brushwork as the epitome of the artist's inner feelings and latent spirituality.

The security guard mused to himself over how many people had passed favourable comments on the painting throughout the day. There were 75 pictures at the exhibition, and he personally wouldn't have given £1 for the lot. He thought they were nothing but a disorganised splash of colour, with wild lines going nowhere. He was not into modern art, himself.

When the exhibition was being set up the previous day he had wandered past the paintings, almost gasping at the price tags of between £15,000 and £150,000. He looked again at the young couple who seemed so enraptured with this last picture.

"£25,000," the girl was saying. "That seems very reasonable for such a touching and emotive balance of bravery and vulnerability that this piece portrays."

The boy peered closely at the bottom right hand corner. "The signature's almost indecipherable," he muttered.

His companion consulted her programme. "It's called 'Turmoil In Heaven,' and according to this, the artist is Roger Barrymore."

"Barrymore?" The young man looked surprised. "It's very different from his other works. There's more depth and clarity of vision in this one than in anything else of his I've seen."

The girl scanned the programme quickly. "It's the only Barrymore here today and it's by far the best picture in the exhibition. Let's go and see if anyone's bought it."

They moved off across the gallery towards the sales office. The security guard breathed a sigh of relief. It was almost closing time. There would be no more visitors to the exhibition now; he could relax.

He walked over to the painting and looked at the signature. He knew the unreadable scrawl did not say Roger Barrymore. The artist's name was Angela Blackshaw. Unhooking the picture, he brought it down, propping it up against the wall.

Then he picked up another picture concealed behind his desk and slotted it on to the empty hook. To him it was just another meaningless tangle of lines and colour. The name on it was clearly distinguishable: Roger Barrymore.

Security guard David Blackshaw carefully wrapped several layers of newspaper around the picture which had been on display all day. He had to be careful getting it home. His nine-year-old daughter, Angela, had insisted she wanted her work back undamaged.

Harvey Looks For A Friend

Harvey the ghost was sad. He wanted a friend to play with, but each time he went to find one everybody ran away.

He didn't mean to scare them, but of course most boys and girls are frightened of ghosts. Harvey tried telling them he wouldn't hurt them, but they were so scared they all hid from him. Being a ghost is no fun at all, he thought.

He was just wondering where he could find a friend when he heard a man whistling round the corner. Quiet at first, but getting louder every second. Then Harvey saw the man. It was Postman Mike, who popped letters through everyone's letterboxes. Everyone's except Harvey's, that is. No-one ever wrote to Harvey.

"Mike's everyone's friend," thought Harvey. "I'm sure he'll be a chum for me."

Postman Mike was a short tubby man with a round jolly face. He wore a cap on his head and always carried a big sack full of letters and birthday cards.

"Postman....postman Mike," called Harvey. "Wait for me, I want you to be my friend."

The postman turned round, saw Harvey the ghost and got the fright of his life. With a yell that could be heard all over town he threw his sack of letters in the air and ran faster than any child ever did in their school race.

"Oh dear," sighed Harvey. "He must have some friends already." Harvey started to cry and a huge shiny tear rolled down his face. He was so lonely.

Then he saw Aaron, the little boy who lived next door. Aaron was skipping down the garden path bouncing a big yellow ball. Harvey loved to play ball.

"Little boy next door," he called as loudly as he could. "Can I play ball with you, please?"

Aaron stopped skipping and his ball stopped bouncing. He looked at Harvey, but like all other little boys and girls he was frightened of ghosts and ran back inside his house. Harvey heard the door close with a loud bang.

"Oh dear," sighed Harvey again. "I wonder why nobody wants to play with me."

Harvey didn't know what to do, so he sat under a tree and cried and cried and cried. He would have probably cried all day if a little bird hadn't flown on to a branch just above his head. It was a robin. His favourite bird. He loved to watch them hopping around the garden and he loved to hear them singing. So he felt a little happier when he looked up and saw it sitting there.

Wiping the tears away, he tried to smile. But he hoped the robin wouldn't see him, because birds were just like the boys and girls – they never wanted to be his friend, either.

Poor Harvey tried to think of all the reasons why nobody would be his pal. He could not understand it. He always tried to be good and kind, because he knew no-one liked mean and nasty boys and girls. He knew if you were naughty and unkind to people you didn't deserve to have any friends. Sometimes he was told off by Mummy Ghost and Daddy Ghost – the last time was when he took some of Mummy Ghost's jam tarts that she had just baked, and the time before that was when he had trampled on Daddy Ghost's flowers in the garden while chasing his ball. But he felt that everyone did something that was just a tiny bit mischievous sometimes, no matter how good they were normally. He didn't think it should stop him having a friend.

Harvey sniffled as he wiped away another tear. There! Now the robin had gone, too, flown away to another tree.

It was nearly teatime and Harvey would have to go home soon. He wished he could find a little playmate to show Mummy Ghost. He sat under the tree for about five more minutes, and was just thinking he would have to go when he saw someone else coming along the road.

"Hello," he shouted. "Will you be my friend?" He recognised this new little boy who lived in the next road.

He was surprised, but ever so happy, when the boy skipped up to him and said: "Yes, I'll be your friend. I'm Raymond the ghost and no-one ever wants to be with me. They always run off when they see me."

"And I'm Harvey the ghost. I think I know now why no-one wants to be play with us. Grown-ups have other grown-ups to talk to. Boys and girls play with other boys and girls. Even the birds in the trees only seem to sing to other birds. But we can play together because we're both ghosts."

Harvey was happy.

He had a friend now.

The Twitter Bully

Foreword:

The Twitter Bully is dedicated to anyone who has been bullied, stalked, harassed or abused in any way on Twitter, or, indeed, on any social media platform.

Originally appearing in Awethology Dark, an anthology published by Plaisted Publishing House Ltd., New Zealand, this 7,300-word fantasy tale ruthlessly explores the devastating consequences that sustained harassment on Twitter have for a young girl, Annie Galway, and how karma exacts a terrifying and horrific revenge on the teenager responsible.

Inspiration came from personal experiences on Twitter. I became so outraged about the behaviour of stalkers and bullies who harassed other users, that I became an active anti-online bully campaigner.

The Twitter Bully

They were the two most terrifying sounds I'd ever heard.

That awful ratcheting as the handcuffs locked around my wrists, securing them uncompromisingly behind my back. And the ominous clang as the thick steel door slammed shut, imprisoning me in this tiny square cell...the walls less than two yards apart.

So here I am, my bare feet freezing on the rough stone floor – yes, my shoes and socks were taken from me as soon as I arrived at this godforsaken place.

I glance up at the clock in the ceiling. I know, weird, isn't it? A clock in the ceiling. It's the only thing in this dimly-lit cell. Apart from me, of course. The clock's telling me I've been here for just over an hour.

I thought she might have freed my hands when she locked me in; I'm not going anywhere or doing anything, am I, incarcerated within these stone walls? But oh no, she just shoved me through that steel door, leaving my hands cuffed behind me.

Again I pull at the short chain keeping them there, but to no avail. In the early moments after that horrendous sound of the door slamming shut and the resounding click of the lock sliding into place, I tried undressing it. You know the manoeuvre, bringing your hands down below your bum and stepping over the chain so your hands are in front of you. Still cuffed closely together, of course, but at least you're not completely helpless as you are when they're secured behind your back.

But there's no chance of that with these cuffs. The chain is too short. It won't get anywhere near passing under my bum.

The next thing I did was take stock of my surroundings. Right, that was done in five seconds flat. Less than six feet of stone wall in every direction.

Not a lot I could do. I tried sitting down with my back pressed up against the wall as much as my restricted arms would allow, but within a few moments it wasn't just my feet that were freezing. That icy floor took almost all the feeling from my bum, with the wall performing the same trick on my back. The only way to get any comfort (and I use the word 'comfort' loosely here) was to keep walking round the cell. The movement jarred my thoughts into action. And pretty unnerving thoughts they were, too.

Surely they'd come for me soon. But what if they didn't? I'd no idea how long they intended to keep me here – wherever 'here' was – and what had that custody sergeant said when she took my shoes and socks? Oh yes: "You won't need footwear where you're going?" What the hell was that supposed to mean?

"Hey, how long am I going to be in here?" I shouted. My words died instantly, swallowed whole by the strange deadening effects of the thick stone surrounding me. And when I say thick, I mean thick. In the few seconds after we arrived at the cell and the door was pushed open, following that walk down the passage in the heart of the rock, I could see the walls were a solid nine inches.

Without my trainers I couldn't even kick the door to try and attract their attention. But I somehow doubted that even if I did kick it, it wouldn't do any good. I reckon the sound would only be audible *inside* the cell, as the steel was every bit as thick as the stone. I'm sure nobody outside would hear a thing. And the door itself... it was exactly that, just a solid door. In all police dramas I've seen on telly, police cell doors have an inspection hatch. This had nothing. It was simply a block of steel. No handle on the inside. No keyhole on the inside either. So even if I could manage to get my hands free, find a paperclip or other piece of wire from somewhere and was an expert lock-picker (which I'm not, by the way), I'd still be in a bigger pickle than a pound of tomatoes.

Okay, I'm trying to put a brave face on it, but I begin to realise how incredibly vulnerable and helpless I am. Locked in a tiny, dark cell. No idea where. No idea how long I'll be here. Barefoot. Hands cuffed securely behind my back. Cold. No, it doesn't come much more vulnerable and daunting than that.

So, as I say, here I am, entering the second hour of my imprisonment. And for what? Because they call me a Twitter bully. Okay, let's scroll back along the timeline to before I was locked in this cell. Further back, to when I still had my shoes and socks on. Even further back, to just before I was handcuffed.

The beef burgers were pretty good in this fast food joint, especially with cheese. We'd all surreptitiously pulled those horrible gherkins out and thrown them on the floor under the table. And, of course, none of the gang would be seen dead with those poncey fish or chicken efforts.

As for the veggie burgers; well! I remembered the time Sasha shot her foot out just as that stuck-up bitch Harriett Bloomfield from Year 11 was coming past with one of those cardboard burgers, as I call them, and tripped her up. Oh, you should have seen it. It was hysterical. Bloomfield's momentum carried her upper body forward while her leg stayed behind. It doesn't take a physics genius to know that such a swiftly executed change in the centre of gravity won't leave the victim in an upright position for long. In Bloomfield's case it was less than two seconds. But it wasn't simply going down, oh no, much better than that. Those deliciously inviting blue eyes of hers widened in horror and she flung her arms out in a vain attempt to regain her balance. That had a rather unfortunate effect on the tray she was carrying, and consequently on the veggie burger, chips and strawberry milkshake which, until that moment, had resided on said tray. Being suddenly devoid of any human contact, they performed their own parabolic arc, staying airborne just long enough for Bloomfield's head to be precisely where gravity dictated they would come to rest.

Her flailing arms did nothing to prevent that pretty face from crashing sickeningly into the floor tiles – and then everything was down on top of the corn-blonde hair, burger and chips and milkshake and all. The corner of the tray did just enough to knock the lid off the polystyrene cup and the thick strawberry drink gushed out to be greeted by a loud cheer and helpless laughter from our gang as it soaked the back of her head.

We were just discussing that little event from a few months ago, and I was taking a noisy slurp of banana milkshake through my straw, when the door burst open and in they marched. Three of them. Two men and a woman. In police uniform. Well, not quite police uniform, but near enough. They headed straight for our table, and the biggest and burliest of the two men – I swear he was at least seven feet tall and weighed 25-stones – looked down at me. That was when I realised it wasn't quite a police uniform. The jackets looked authentic enough, although what the TPD badge on the left breast stood for, I had no idea. I do now. Each 'officer' had a telescopic truncheon tucked into a pouch in their belt, along with a pair of handcuffs.

It's the trousers the belts were supporting that gave the game away. They were all wearing denim jeans which, as far as I was aware were not standard police issue. Nor were the Kobe Aston Martin sneakers, even if they'd been the cheaper ones at £338 a pair, which these definitely weren't – these were the Hyperdunks at £770. Jesus, if these were real police it's no wonder the force is having to make cuts. How else could they fund shoes like these?

I looked up into his face. "Good evening, occifer." I thought maybe the bravado humour would make that granite face crack into a smile. "I'm not drunk – it's just that sometimes I get my 'c's and 'f's mixed up. Not as bad, though, as my friend called Ynot. Well, actually, it's Tony, but he's dyslexic." No, the granite didn't crack.

But it spoke: "Are you Tyler Conway?" The voice was as hard as its owner's face, the words booming across the room. A hush descended on the fast food joint as everyone turned to look.

I swallowed nervously. But this had to be a joke, didn't it? I mean, these weren't real police. "Have you put them up to this?" I asked, turning to my friends. But I could tell by their faces they hadn't. It had to be a joke though.

"Are. You. Tyler. Conway?" Granite asked again, each word distinctly defined, with too long a pause between each one.

Yeah, it's a joke, surely. "Yep. That's me. Got it in one, occifer. It's a fair cop." I held my hands out six inches apart, in the time-honoured jest. "Slap the bracelets on me."

It was all over before I hardly realised it had begun. Granite grabbed my left hand, hauling me to my feet and spinning me round. The other 'policeman' slammed my head down on to the neighbouring table, while their female colleague twisted my right hand behind my back. And there was that sound I mentioned earlier; the ratcheting noise as the steel closed over my wrist. Granite forced my other hand behind my back to meet the same fate, and within a couple of seconds I was hauled upright by the hair, pulling in vain against the handcuffs that ensured I was a helpless prisoner.

My friends had all been quietly sniggering up to that point, probably thinking, like me, that this was all some sort of joke. But after that little episode of my head cracking painfully on to the table they fell ominously silent.

"Tyler Conway." It was the 'policewoman' this time. "I'm arresting you on suspicion of Twitter bullying, harassment and trolling. From this moment forward, you have absolutely no rights, either in the real world or the cyber world. Do you understand me?"

Well, I certainly didn't understand. And judging by the stunned, blank looks of everyone else in the fast food joint, neither did they.

"What? No, of course I don't. What's all this about? What's going on?"

I heard whispers from a neighbouring table: "Twitter bully? How disgusting."

The policewoman was speaking again: "Tyler Conway, it is my duty to take you to a place of custody where you will be tried and judged for your alleged crimes against innocent Twitter users."

This was getting ridiculous. I half expected her to read me my rights. Ah, no, what was it she'd just said? – I had no rights in the real or cyber worlds.

What? Not even a "whatever you tweet will be typed up in 280 characters and may be tweeted against you"?

Nope, I guess not.

She turned away, spinning on her heel, to face the door. "Bring him."

I started to say something about my hoody slung over the back of my chair, but then thought about the rather illegal contents of two of the pockets. Best to leave it here. The gang'll look after it.

Granite gripped my right elbow, the other policeman my left and they marched me after her. As I stumbled towards the exit I saw the diners' horrified faces staring up at me. But were they horrified for my fate, or by what these 'police officers' said I'd done?

Seconds later we were outside in the car park. A large white van nestled up against the pavement a few paces from the door, and I could see a very familiar logo on the side. But the logo wasn't displayed just once – a whole row of blue birds in flight adorned the vehicle. And above them, in huge blue letters: TPD. I barely had time to register this before they dragged me to the rear doors. Granite inserted a key into the lock and pulled them both open.

A light came on automatically, illuminating a stark white interior devoid of anything except a metal seat running the length of the left-hand side. The policewoman headed to the front of the van, leaving me alone with Granite and the other guy, who I hadn't heard speak up to this point. As they thrust me up the single step and pushed me inside I noticed three short links of chain attached to a steel ring set in the seat, and a longer chain fastened to a ring bolted into the floor.

Now the silent one spoke. "Over here, Conway, and sit down." He guided me, none-too-gently, it has to be said, to the seat and forced me down on it, before producing two padlocks from the pouch on his belt. Reaching behind me, I felt the unrelenting steel of the handcuffs bite deeper into my wrists as he padlocked them to the chain.

I was too stunned to speak, and before I knew it, he had stooped down to my feet, wrapping the floor chain twice around my ankles, cinching it between them, finally securing it with the remaining padlock. I couldn't move my hands or feet more than an inch.

The grin on their faces as they retreated to the back of the van filled me with dread. But perhaps not so much dread as Granite's words did. "I hope you went to the toilet at that burger place. You're going to be chained there for quite some time, and there are no toilet stops on this journey."

They stepped out of the van and the doors clanged shut. Immediately I was engulfed by pitch blackness. Then the sound of the door lock clicked into place.

A few seconds later I heard another door slam – presumably as Granite and Man-Of-Few-Words settled into their seats alongside the woman – then the engine fired up and I felt us move away.

I pulled at my shackles. Not only were my hands held tightly behind my back, they were now firmly anchored to the seat as well. Likewise my feet were locked together and secured to the floor.

As I sat there, completely helpless, waiting for my eyes to adjust to the dark, I felt a vibration through the metal panels as the vehicle increased speed. The adjustment to the dark was a long time coming, I thought. In fact it never did come. Not a chink of light could be seen anywhere. The interior of this TPD van in which I was now held prisoner was in absolute pitch blackness. I had never experienced anything like it. And to say it was frightening and unnerving was an understatement in the extreme. For the first time in my life I was not in control. Not only that, but someone else had total control, total power, over me. I didn't know who they were, nor why they're doing this to me. Surely they were not treating me like this because I'd upset a few people on Twitter. As I sat there, unable to do absolutely anything except think, I couldn't be sure if my thoughts were getting increasingly more rational or more irrational.

I could sit this out, I mused, if I just played ignorant. After all, how could they (whoever 'they' are), know that I'm a well-practiced, chapter-and-verse Twitter bully? My personal Twitter account, TylerBConway747, with @SuperTyler user name, was absolutely squeaky clean. It was only in my other guise of MrEviL that I conducted my unrelenting bullying, harassment and trolling. Hiding behind anonymity, I was completely safe from detection and free to cause upset and torment galore. Oh, how I loved to think what those poor stupid saps went through every time @evilreigns popped up in their mentions.

But again, I thought, treating me this way was like cracking the proverbial walnut with the proverbial sledgehammer. Okay, so I may have upset a few (few?? For 'few,' read 'many') people on Twitter, but was that any reason to chain me up like an animal? Did I really deserve this?

The really worrying thing was, though, that I didn't actually think this was a genuine, pukka, police van, nor my captors genuine, pukka occifers of the law.

I had absolutely no idea how long I sat there; the enforced immobility causing my muscles to scream silently, but urgently, at me. "Move us," they urged. "Move us. We're cramping up." Yes, okay, I wish I could – but it was several hours ago that my cuffed hands were secured to the bench and my feet chained to the floor, and I could do diddly squat about it.

Hold on, what's this? The van's stopped. I strained my ears and heard the front doors slam, rocking the vehicle a little. The next sound was the clink of the rear door lock sliding back and then a slab of light flooded in. Screwing my eyes tightly shut to combat the painful brightness, I just caught a glimpse of Granite and Man-Of-Few-Words silhouetted outside, then heard, rather than saw, them make their way into my prison. I felt their hands opening the padlocks that held me securely to the bench and floor. My feet were now free of their shackles, but my hands remained securely cuffed behind my back. Without a word the none-too-dynamic-duo hauled me up, my muscles now screaming in protest at their sudden call to action after my hours of restrained captivity.

With Granite gripping my right arm tightly and painfully, and M-O-F-W my left, I was manhandled down the rear step, coming face to face with the 'policewoman' who seemed to be in charge.

The vehicle was parked a few metres from a somewhat gothic-looking building. The two-storey imposing stone structure looming up in front of me had turrets topping semi-circular towers at both ends of the frontage, connected by a castellated strip. Huge arched double doors, which wouldn't have looked out of place behind a castle portcullis, were flanked on both sides by two dark fathomless windows. Immediately above the doors a strip ran the width of the building showing the blue flying Twitter bird at either end, sandwiching large ornate lettering spelling out the legend: Twitter Police Department.

Aha. TPD. Gottit.

Now here's another mystery. It had been getting dusk when I was dragged into the van, and although I was imprisoned there for several hours, it didn't feel as if the whole night and half a day had passed. Yet here I was, standing in broad daylight with the sun blazing high in the sky. This couldn't be England, though, surely. Judging from the heat we were in Death Valley. And my surroundings didn't argue very powerfully against that, either. The mountainous landscape was utterly barren. The ground in the immediate vicinity was nothing but a cracked, rocky wasteland. No road! And yet I hadn't felt any bumping as the vehicle had apparently been nearing its destination. It looked as if the building could actually have grown out of the very mountain it stood against. Its uneven stone blocks appeared to match colour and texture perfectly. If the mountain had indeed given birth to this building, it was the parent of an only child. There was no other structure in sight.

"Right," she snapped. "Bring him inside. Let's get this over with, we're needed in the field again."

My 'helpers' guided me up the steps and through those gigantic oak doors into a huge vaulted waiting area. I say 'waiting area' but there's no-one waiting now; just row upon row of empty, red leather seats. There must be at least 50 of them. And at the far end of the room another 'policewoman' sat behind a reception hatch, above which a sign proclaimed this to be the Twitter Police Department Custody Suite. As they frogmarched me towards her I saw a smile creeping across her rosebud lips and dark hazel eyes in equal measure. But there was something decidedly unsettling about it, almost malicious, as if she relished the moment, savouring the foretaste of something which she would clearly enjoy and I clearly wouldn't.

She looked me straight in the eye as I arrived in front of her, then glanced down at a computer screen set into the counter. As she did so, I couldn't help but be captivated by the sheen of her hair, the colour of which matched those 'come-to-bed' eyes perfectly. And I caught a combined whiff of her perfume and shampoo.

"Tyler Conway." Her honeyed tones positively purred my name.

Here was a chick to die for.

When all this is over I'm coming back here of my own free will to ask her out. I wonder what her Twitter handle is. I looked to her perfectly rounded left breast (but only, you understand, because that's where her name badge was strategically located, identifying her as 'Custody Sergeant Aimee Crystal).

"Tyler Conway?" She purred my name again, but this time the inflection indicating a question rather than a statement.

I nodded enthusiastically. "That's me, Aimee. Good to see you."

She looked across at Granite and M-O-F-W, each of whom was still painfully gripping my arms. "Okay boys, bring him through." As she reached beneath the counter, presumably to press a button, I heard the click of a magnetised lock being released, and a door alongside her moved a fraction of an inch. Granite pushed it open, his pull on my arm strongly suggesting I go through. Once I was over the threshold and inside her small office beyond, she spun her swivel chair to face me.

"Possessions." Granite interpreted her solitary word as a command and his hands started sweeping my body, pausing to remove my wallet and house keys from the back pocket of my jeans, and phone from my shirt pocket. I shudder to think what would happen if they'd found my flick knife and packet of white powder. But they were safely in my hoody, which the gang were hopefully guarding with their lives.

Then Granite's hands were at my groin. "Oi," I began. "What..."

"Shut it."

Okay, I relaxed... well, relaxed as much as this whole scenario would allow, realising that he was simply confiscating my belt.

Aimee put my wallet, keys, phone and belt into a plastic tray.

"Thank you," she said to Granite and M-O-F-W. "I'll take him from here." After they retreated back into the waiting area she pressed two buttons. One resealed the door, the other brought a steel shutter down, covering her reception hatch. We were alone.

I tried bravado again. "Okay, you've got my belt, phone, wallet and keys. What more do you want from me?"

If she saw my wink, she ignored it, and simply fixed me with what I can only describe as a smile that contained malice, mischief and a smirk all rolled into one. Although it lit up her face, it was for her benefit rather than mine.

"Well, now you ask," she said, "I need your shoes and socks. Take them off."

"What?"

"You heard. Your shoes and socks. Take them off."

"Why?"

"You won't need footwear where you're going." Her voice grew stern now: "Take them off."

I spun round to show her my hands were still securely cuffed behind my back, and rattled the chain for good measure.

"That might be quite difficult, given my current circumstances," I said. As I turned back towards her, her movement was so sudden I never saw it coming. I don't know if it was her fist or a slap, but the force with which her hand struck my left cheek sent me staggering into the wall.

"I won't ask you again, Conway. Off. Now."

With my face stinging like fury I managed to lever both my trainers off from the heel, with the toes of my opposite foot, then squatted down to peel my socks off from the ankle.

"See, it wasn't that hard, was it?" she said, scooping them up and depositing them in the plastic tray, before putting everything into a locker behind her.

The next few moments saw me following her through a door at the rear of the small office and down a long set of quite steep, rough and cold, stone steps. At the bottom a narrow passage stretched away with a pronounced downward slope.

The floor comprised the same stone as the walls and ceiling. If I'd still been wearing shoes I doubt I'd have noticed the transition from the smooth white floor tiles in her office, but without shoes I winced as every step brought the vulnerable soles of my bare feet into contact with the stone's jagged roughness. Every so often the intense sharpness caused me to stumble, and without the use of my hands to correct my balance, the equally rough walls managed to graze my elbows and face. If I didn't know better I'd say that confiscating my shoes ahead of being led down this passage was designed specifically to make the trip as unpleasant and uncomfortable as possible. Actually, come to think about it, I don't think I did know any better.

Eventually we came to that nine inch thick steel door where Aimee and I parted company.

And now, here I am, beginning the second hour of my imprisonment in this tiny, uncomfortable cell.

"When are you going to realise you've got the wrong person?" I scream. "Let me out, now! If you don't release me I'll sue your asses off." Realising how lame that sounds I rattle the handcuff chain furiously – the only action I can take in my current state of impotent helplessness, to be in any way rebellious.

Again I think fleetingly of kicking the door, but am put off by the fact that nine inch thick steel will emerge victorious in a battle with bare feet any day of the week. I really am totally helpless in here. And I don't like it one little bit.

Whoaahh! That takes me by surprise.

I'm definitely not expecting a soft female voice to call my name. And it's coming from the clock! I mentioned the clock in the ceiling, didn't I? It's 18 inches square, and although the time is shown with two hands in analogue format, the display actually looks like it's created digitally. And there's that voice again. Yep, it's definitely coming from the clock.

"Tyler Conway." As well as broadcasting that well-modulated voice into the tiny cell, the clock is also doing something else decidedly funny. No, I don't mean it's reciting the Dead Parrot sketch or showing a scene from Mrs Doubtfire – that would be funny ha ha and this is definitely funny peculiar.

Jagged lines, almost like cracks and splinters in the glass, flicker across the clock face, obscuring the hands and numbers. As the lines begin to dissipate again, a face emerges behind them.

Oh. My. God. Now I start to tremble.

What I now see on that digital screen shakes me to my very core and tells me that maybe these guys are serious after all. My heart sinks as

I realise that pleading ignorance of my MrEviL tweets just isn't going to cut the mustard.

Fading into view, as all but four of the lines fade out of view, is a pale, somewhat wan-looking heart-shaped face with a slightly snub (but cute, nevertheless, it has to be said) nose. But the eyes! Oh, dear God, the eyes! It was those eyes on the Photoshopped image that had first attracted me to this Twitter account during one of my regular trolling sessions. The eyes had been replaced with jet black holes, also heart-shaped (I remember wondering at that time what was it about this person that they were so into hearts. Especially black ones).

Yes, I've seen this face many times before. But only when using my MrEviL @evilreigns account. It's Annie Galway's Twitter avatar. And I clearly remember my last tweet to her yesterday: '@Anngal01 Go hang urself, u fat cow. Actually don't. ur weight will snap the rope.'

Four jagged slashes continue to scar the screen in a slight diagonal pattern, as Annie's avatar grows in strength and stature, taking up residence behind them. Those deep, penetrating heart-shaped black holes bore into my eyes, and the blackness of the lips accentuates their firm set, hardening just a fraction more. And as I move from the centre of the cell to press up against the wall, those black holes follow me. Not like in paintings where the eyes only seem to move. The intelligence behind these holes continues to stare straight at me, chilling my bone marrow a thousand times more than the icy stone of my prison could ever do.

And what's happening now? Not only the face, but the entire square housing it, pushes forward through the remaining slashes, breaking free of the clock and coming into the physical reality of the cell. For a second it simply hovers there, near the ceiling, before floating down until those black holes are level with my eyes.

The black lips part to form my name again. It's that same well-modulated voice I heard before.

For God's sake, Annie Galway's avatar is talking to me.

131

"Tyler Conway, you have been called here to answer for your crimes of cyberbullying. Today you will face the consequences of your bullying, trolling and harassment of innocent Twitter users."

For once I'm struck dumb. Usually I can hide behind my anonymous MrEviL name and skull and crossbones avatar. But the bravado which that usually brings, now deserts me as I look into those dark, piercing holes. How could I feel smaller, more vulnerable and helpless than I did a few moments ago? I don't know, but I sure as hell do.

What! No way could she have read my thoughts. Could she? No. It has to be coincidence. Doesn't it? But her words are taken almost verbatim, directly from my brain: "Tyler Conway, you are feeling extremely vulnerable right now. You are a helpless prisoner locked in a tiny cell. Your hands fastened securely behind your back serve to emphasise and heighten your captivity. You are barefoot, battered, bruised, grazed and bleeding. Someone else is in control; you have no power to stop them. You have no power to do anything at all. You don't know what's going to happen next. You feel as if your very essence as a human being has been totally and utterly violated."

Yep. That sums it up to a tee.

"Tyler Conway, what you're feeling now is what your bullying and harassment inflicts on other people. On me. Your MrEviL tweets as @evilreigns cause people to suffer... they feel helpless, powerless, violated, battered. You wreck their lives, Tyler Conway, like you wrecked mine, Your final tweet to me ended my life. I couldn't take your persistent bullying and harassment any more, and I did what you told me to do. I hanged myself. But the rope didn't snap."

Her square avatar, just inches from my face, tilts upwards, directing those black bottomless pits to the ceiling. I follow her gaze. My last tweet is now showing in the clock.

Okaaay, yeah, I said that, and why not? I may be helpless and vulnerable in this cell, but I reckon attack is still my best form of defence. So the stupid cow's dead. "And that's my fault, how?" I retort. "This is my Twitter account. I can comment on what I like, say what I like, and no-one can stop me. I'm glad you're dead, you stupid cow."

The avatar remains inscrutable as a number of my other tweets aimed at her scroll through the clock: 'u fat cow, u stink. U'll never get a boyfriend. No-one'll ever want u.' 'Ur just a useless lump of meat, writhing with maggots.'

I look at the first half dozen, then turn my eyes away.

"So?" I snarl. "My Twitter account, my rules. You blocked me ages ago, how do you know about these tweets, anyway, unless you're trolling me? Stalking me?"

Her only response is to whisper: "Twitter bully guilty." And again: "Twitter bully guilty." And again. And again.

The jagged slashes cover the clock once more, before another avatar breaks through and floats down. Oh, this'll be good. It's that donkey who runs what used to be my favourite TV programme.

This time, as well as my tweets about him scroll down the clock face, the donkey narrates them for me, too. Just to make sure I get the message, I suppose. Well, that makes sense, as he can never get the message across in his programme. A few of my choice phrases shine through: 'Incompetent turd.' 'Nasty, pathetic little prat.' 'Can't write a decent character to save his life.' 'I'm coming after ur children.' 'U're ded. And so are ur children.'

And all the time his thin, whining voice is accompanied by Annie Galway's incessant whispering: "Twitter bully guilty. Twitter bully guilty."

The clock face clouds with the jagged, diagonal slashes again as he obviously reaches the end of his episode. He now joins Annie's whispering. They're both at it in perfect unison: "Twitter bully guilty. Twitter bully guilty."

Oh, for goodness sake, who's this coming through the clock now? Yes, there's no mistaking that nose. It's that little tart three years below me at school. She, too, narrates the tweets I sent to her as they scroll along the clockface. I remember those tweets well: 'That nose! What an ugly lump of clay.' 'You'd be better looking after washing your face in acid.'

And that insidious whispering all the time in the background: "Twitter bully guilty, Twitter bully guilty."

Now she finishes, and her avatar congregates with Annie and the donkey in the corner of my cell. Three voices chanting: "Twitter bully guilty, Twitter bully guilty."

Harriett Bloomfield comes next. 'Stuck up cow.' 'Can't keep away from the boys, can u?'

Many more tweets.

Many more avatars.

I've no idea how long this goes on for, but there must be at least 30 avatars crowding my cell now. A few choice tweets stand out: 'I've got pictures of your kids,' 'tweeting your private phone number shortly.' 'You're a child abuser.' 'Do you really do that with your daughter?' 'Your child's just a cretin, never mind that she's autistic.'

And all the while there's that combined and insistent, throbbing, whispered chant in the background. It's actually quite hypnotic: "Twitter bully guilty, Twitter bully guilty." Never changing pitch, never changing tone, never changing volume. In some tacky horror novel the whispering would get increasingly louder, raising to a crescendo, and because of my cuffed hands I wouldn't be able to cover my ears to drown out the sound as it burrows through my eardrums and into my brain, teetering me over the brink into madness. No, there's none of that here – just an incessant, never-changing whisper: "Twitter bully guilty, Twitter bully guilty."

What? Oh no. I might have guessed that sanctimonious old fruitloop would stick his oar in. He just can't leave us alone, despite the threats we've all made against him. I watch helplessly as Byron Carruthers' smug avatar slips through the clock. I've seen enough of these Twitter profile pictures in the last few hours to know exactly when those eyes will come alive.

Carruthers' rugged face, topped and tailed by thinning grey hair and a grey designer stubble goatee, floats down gently to the same level as mine. And there they go, the dark brown eyes peering over the top of his glasses, suddenly shine and sparkle.

What was I saying earlier about attack being my best form of defence? Well, here I go again.

"I'm not listening to a word you say. This is what I think of you and your interfering." With that, I spit a thick, glutinous glob of phlegm straight at him, watching with glee as it slowly trickles down his cyber nose and over his cyber mouth. I don't know if either he or his avatar even notice my act of defiance as there's certainly no change in his expression, and his voice is quiet, measured and calm.

"I have links and associations with several international groups fighting online bullying," he says. "A number of them have been watching Tyler Conway's anonymous Twitter account, MrEviL, for the last year. He and a small clique of followers are renowned for vile cyber attacks, sustained trolling, harassment and subtweeting.

"When anti-bully activists intervene on behalf of his victims, they, too, have been subjected to a torrent of organised abuse and threats. In a bid to discredit anyone opposing their bullying, Conway and his acolytes regularly spread wild and malicious lies, urging their followers to block anti-bully campaigners. Many innocent and gullible followers simply believe the spoon-fed lies instead of seeking the truth for themselves.

"And when a number of people finally realised the scale and malicious ferocity of lies directed at the personal life of one renowned anti-bully ambassador, Conway tweeted: 'Anyone defending him in any way, shape or form, will be blocked instantly.'"

I glance up at the clock screen to see that particular tweet scrolling through. Then Carruthers is talking again.

"Before we can begin to understand a cyber bully's mentality and psyche we must first take a look at the code they live by – their bible, or their national anthem:

'**Baa Baa Bleat Bleat, have you any bile?**
Yes Sir, Yes Sir, we spread it all the while.
We take a lie from our Master, push it far and wide,
And wash away the truth with the outgoing tide.

**Lies and hate we spread 'til our victims fill with dread,
We care not a jot that justice shall be dead.'**

"Online bullying is every bit as powerful as physical bullying and its consequences are just as terrifying. The problem is that people on Twitter and Facebook hide behind anonymity – these keyboard bullies know that it'll take quite a lot of cyber detecting to find the stone they crawl under.

"Most online bullying, stalking and harassment begins with taking those lies from their Master – whatever they conceive that Master to be, whether it's an external influence or their own internal demons urging them on, and then wreaking havoc upon innocent people's lives.

"The alliance of anti-bully activists decided that Tyler Conway had finally gone too far when his tweet to Annie Galway was the direct cause of her taking her own life."

Carruthers pauses as my damning tweet appears on the clockface again. That self-righteous prat certainly knows how to create effect, I'll give him that.

'@Anngal01 Go hang urself, u fat cow. Actually don't. ur weight will snap the rope.'

Suddenly all is quiet around me. That intolerable whispering ceases. The only sound now is my own breathing. But the hostility in the eyes of those silent avatars is all-too-evident as they glare at me, seemingly from every inch of the cell.

I swallow.

And again. My throat is as dry as a bone.

"Tyler Conway." Somehow I sense a note of doom-laden finality in the way Annie Galway's avatar utters my name. "You have been found guilty of the Twitter crime of bullying and harassment. Do you have anything to say before I pass sentence?"

My parched throat is reluctant to let me speak, but eventually I force the lie out.

"I didn't mean to upset anyone."

Am I really saying this? Of course I meant to upset them. But before I can lie further I'm dimly aware of Annie uttering one word: "I…"

That's the whole point of MrEviL, isn't it?

Another solitary word from Annie: "…sentence…"

My other persona, not one that I could publicly acknowledge as being the real Tyler Conway (Annie again: "…you…") was created to do just that. To bully other Twitter users for the sheer fun, the sheer hell, of it,

Annie: "…to…"

to harass them, no matter how much they ask me to stop – and when those polite requests turn to heartfelt begging; well, that was music to my ears, manna from heaven,

"…eternity…"

as I ignored them and increased my harassment. And as for that sanctimonious, holier-than-thou, anti-bully campaigner Byron Carruthers,

"…in…"

well, I'm just glad I forced that do-gooder off Twitter for a while with those brilliant lies about him. That worked so much better than I could have dared hope for.

"…Twitter…"

Bullies should unite against him and his ilk – interfering busybodies, the lot of them.

"…Hell…

If the people we bully can't stand the heat they should get the hell out of the Twitter kitchen.

WHAT? It's just struck me what Annie said: "I sentence you to eternity in Twitter Hell." What's that supposed to mean?

An avatar breaks free from the circle surrounding me, suddenly diving to my feet. At its first touch my feet and ankles feel as if they're exploding in a torrent of boiling oil, the skin starting to melt and peel away, exposing red raw flesh beneath. A glimpse of white bone peeps through.

A scream suddenly rents the air. A scream of absolute horror, terror and pain all rolled into one heart-breaking sound of torment.

Then I realise where that scream now assaulting my ears is coming from. It's coming from me, getting louder and louder, as if the intense sound can dull the increasing, heightening, concentrated pain.

Pain, absolute sheer, undiluted pain. I dance around the cell, every step leaving bloody prints on the stone. With that agonising pain and my balance impaired by my cuffed hands, my frenzied movements accidentally bring my left elbow into contact with the still and silent mob of avatars, instantly refocusing attention away from my burning feet. My arm feels as if it's joined them in that growing cauldron of boiling oil.

A second avatar breaks free from the circle, latching itself onto my chest, burrowing its way inside.

The front of my shirt disintegrates, fragments of material fusing with the now molten gloop of tissue that just a few seconds ago comprised my upper torso.

A third avatar takes my groin.

My legs fall victim to a fourth, and my right arm to a fifth. The agony is intense, intolerable, unrelenting.

Then, the last thing I ever see is Annie leading the remaining avatars to my head. My hair singes for a fraction of a second before bursting into flames as every single avatar smothers my face.

The popping sound I hear is my eyeballs exploding.

Then there is no sound at all. My eardrums have simply melted.

There is no sight.

No sound.

No taste – my tongue melted three seconds ago, but to be honest I hadn't even noticed it, due to the pain consuming every other part of my being.

There is no smell, my olfactory organs having gone the same way as my tongue.

But one sense remains. I haven't been deprived of the ability to feel excruciating, white hot, unfathomable, blistering pain.

My body has gone. All that is left of the human being that was once Tyler Conway – and, yes, I was human, despite the fact that I was acknowledged as a vile, malicious Twitter bully, troll and exponent of harassment – is now an ethereal avatar of intense, agonising, unbearable, intolerable pain which I simply can't take any more.

How long will it last, I wonder?

Then I remember the length of the sentence Annie, my final victim, imposed on me.

Eternity.

THE END

About the Author

Stewart Bint is a novelist, magazine columnist and PR writer. He lives with his wife, Sue, in Leicestershire in the UK, and has two grown-up children, Christopher and Charlotte.

While writing, his office companion is his charismatic budgie, Alfie, or his neighbour's cat. But not at the same time.

When not writing, he can often be found hiking barefoot on woodland trails.

Connect with Stewart Bint Online:

Website:
http://www.stewartbintauthor.weebly.com/
Blog:
www.stewartbintauthor.weebly.com/stewart-bints-blog
Twitter:
Twitter.com/@AuthorSJB
Facebook:
https://www.facebook.com/StewartBintAuthor
Amazon:
https://www.amazon.co.uk/Stewart-Bint/e/B00D18IARS

Printed in Great Britain
by Amazon